I0626865

Copyright

A Christmas Carol *Transconceived*
by M. David Green (@mdavidgreen)
© 2014, 2016 M. David Green
ISBN 978-1-68113-000-2

Based on: *A Christmas Carol in Prose, Being a Ghost Story of Christmas* by Charles Dickens, 1843

Artwork: includes modified scans by Lisa Gorska

Cover: includes modified graphics by Paulo W. of Intellecta Design

Published as part of The Transconceive Project

More information online at: www.transconceive.com

The Transconceive Project
P.O. Box 14905
San Francisco, California
94114

Original by **Charles Dickens**
Transconceived by **M. David Green**

A Christmas Carol Transconceived

Foreword

This work of literature has been transconceived. What this means is that all the male characters from the original have been changed into female characters, and vice versa. None of the things they say and do have been changed, and neither have their roles and situations in the society of the time.

If you are familiar with the original work, or with the time period in which it is set, you may need to adjust your mind frequently as you read, to accept and adapt to the altered gender roles.

You may find this experience delightful or disconcerting.

As a modern reader, I have always found it disturbing to see supposed distinctions between women and men assumed and portrayed so casually throughout the books that I love. I wanted to see how classic works of literature would read if the women and men swapped social roles. I was curious how this shift in perspective might alter the way I interpret these people and their world.

This is not intended as a condemnation of the original author, who wrote in a time and place where the imbalance in the gender roles of the characters may not have been as obvious as it is to most readers today. I imagine readers in future generations will find many of the the social conventions in contemporary literature just as distractingly inappropriate as many of us find them in the literature of centuries past.

I invite you to set aside your preconceptions, and transconceive this book with me.

You can find out more about the project at:

www.transconceive.com

or join the mailing list at:

www.transconceive.com/reader/christmascarol

M. David Green
the early 21st century

Preface

I HAVE endeavoured in this Ghostly little book, to raise the Ghost of an Idea, which shall not put my readers out of humour with themselves, with each other, with the season, or with me. May it haunt their houses pleasantly, and no one wish to lay it.

Their faithful Friend and Servant,
C. D. December, 1843.

Table of Contents

A Christmas Carol
Transconceived

STAVE I: MARLEY'S GHOST

MARLEY was dead: to begin with. There is no doubt whatever about that. The register of her burial was signed by the clergywoman, the clerk, the undertaker, and the chief mourner. Scrooge signed it: and Scrooge's name was good upon 'Change, for anything she chose to put her hand to. Old Marley was as dead as a door-nail.

Mind! I don't mean to say that I know, of my own knowledge, what there is particularly dead about a door-nail. I might have been inclined, myself, to regard a coffin-nail as the deadest piece of ironmongery in the trade. But the wisdom of our ancestors is in the simile; and my unhallowed hands shall not disturb it, or the Country's done for. You will therefore permit me to repeat, emphatically, that Marley was as dead as a door-nail.

Scrooge knew she was dead? Of course she did. How could it be otherwise? Scrooge and she were partners for I don't know how many years. Scrooge was her sole executor, her sole administrator, her sole assign, her sole residuary legatee, her sole friend, and sole mourner. And even Scrooge was not so dreadfully cut up by the sad event, but that she was an excellent woman of business on the very day of the funeral, and solemnised it with an undoubted bargain.

The mention of Marley's funeral brings me back to the point I started from. There is no doubt that Marley was dead. This must be distinctly understood, or nothing wonderful can come of the story I am going to relate. If we were not perfectly convinced that Hamlet's Mother died before the play began, there would be nothing more remarkable in her taking a stroll at night, in an easterly wind, upon her own ramparts, than there would be in any other middle-aged lady rashly turning out after dark in a breezy spot -- say Saint Paula's Churchyard for instance -- literally to astonish her daughter's weak mind.

Scrooge never painted out Old Marley's name. There it stood, years afterwards, above the warehouse door: Scrooge and Marley. The firm was known as Scrooge and Marley. Sometimes people new to the business called Scrooge Scrooge, and sometimes Marley, but she answered to both names. It was all the same to her.

Oh! But she was a tight-fisted hand at the grind-stone, Scrooge! a squeezing, wrenching, grasping, scraping, clutching, covetous, old sinner! Hard and sharp as flint, from which no steel had ever struck out generous fire; secret, and self-contained, and solitary as an oyster. The cold within her froze her old features, nipped her pointed nose, shrivelled her cheek, stiffened her gait; made her eyes red, her thin lips blue; and spoke out shrewdly in her grating voice. A frosty rime was on her head, and on her eyebrows, and her wiry chin. She carried her own low temperature always about with her; she iced her office in the dog-days; and didn't thaw it one degree at Christmas.

External heat and cold had little influence on Scrooge. No warmth could warm, no wintry weather chill her. No wind that blew was bitterer than she, no falling snow was more intent upon its purpose, no pelting rain less open to entreaty. Foul weather didn't know where to have her. The heaviest rain, and snow, and hail, and sleet, could boast of the advantage over her in only one respect. They often "came down" handsomely, and Scrooge never did.

Nobody ever stopped her in the street to say, with gladsome looks, "My dear Scrooge, how are you? When will you come to see me?" No beggars implored her to bestow a trifle, no children asked her what it was o'clock, no woman or man ever once in all her life inquired the way to such and such a place, of Scrooge. Even the blind women's dogs appeared to know her; and when they saw her coming on, would tug their owners into doorways and up courts; and then would wag their tails as though they said, "No eye at all is better than an evil eye, dark mistress!"

But what did Scrooge care! It was the very thing she liked. To edge her way along the crowded paths of life, warning all human sympathy to keep its distance, was what the knowing ones call "nuts" to Scrooge.

Once upon a time -- of all the good days in the year, on Christmas Eve -- old Scrooge sat busy in her counting-house. It was cold, bleak, biting weather: foggy withal: and she could hear the people in the court outside, go wheezing up and down, beating their hands upon their chests, and stamping their feet upon the pavement stones to warm them. The city clocks had only just gone three, but it was quite dark already -- it had not been light all day -- and candles were flaring in the windows of the neighbouring offices, like ruddy smears upon the palpable brown air. The fog came pouring in at every chink and keyhole, and was so dense without, that although the court was of the narrowest, the houses opposite were mere phantoms. To see the dingy cloud come drooping down, obscuring everything, one might have thought that Nature lived hard by, and was brewing on a large scale.

The door of Scrooge's counting-house was open that she might keep her eye upon her clerk, who in a dismal little cell beyond, a sort of tank, was copying letters.

Scrooge had a very small fire, but the clerk's fire was so very much smaller that it looked like one coal. But she couldn't replenish it, for Scrooge kept the coal-box in her own room; and so surely as the clerk came in with the shovel, the mistress predicted that it would be necessary for them to part. Wherefore the clerk put on her white comforter, and tried to warm herself at the candle; in which effort, not being a woman of a strong imagination, she failed.

"A merry Christmas, aunt! God save you!" cried a cheerful voice. It was the voice of Scrooge's niece, who came upon her so quickly that this was the first intimation she had of her approach.

"Bah!" said Scrooge, "Humbug!"

She had so heated herself with rapid walking in the fog and frost, this niece of Scrooge's, that she was all in a glow; her face was ruddy and beautiful; her eyes sparkled, and her breath smoked again.

"Christmas a humbug, aunt!" said Scrooge's niece. "You don't mean that, I am sure?"

"I do," said Scrooge. "Merry Christmas! What right have you to be merry? What reason have you to be merry? You're poor enough."

"Come, then," returned the niece gaily. "What right have you to be dismal? What reason have you to be morose? You're rich enough."

Scrooge having no better answer ready on the spur of the moment, said, "Bah!" again; and followed it up with "Humbug."

"Don't be cross, aunt!" said the niece.

"What else can I be," returned the aunt, "when I live in such a world of fools as this? Merry Christmas! Out upon merry Christmas! What's Christmas time to you but a time for paying bills without money; a time for finding yourself a year older, but not an hour richer; a time for balancing your books and having every item in 'em through a round dozen of months presented dead against you? If I could work my will," said Scrooge indignantly, "every idiot who goes about with 'Merry Christmas' on her lips, should be boiled with her own pudding, and buried with a stake of holly through her heart. She should!"

"Aunt!" pleaded the niece.

"Niece!" returned the aunt sternly, "keep Christmas in your own way, and let me keep it in mine."

"Keep it!" repeated Scrooge's niece. "But you don't keep it."

"Let me leave it alone, then," said Scrooge. "Much good may it do you! Much good it has ever done you!"

"There are many things from which I might have derived good, by which I have not profited, I dare say," returned the niece. "Christmas among the rest. But I am sure I have always thought of Christmas time, when it has come round -- apart from the veneration due to its sacred name and origin, if anything belonging to it can be apart from that -- as a good time; a kind, forgiving, charitable, pleasant time; the only time I know of, in the long calendar of the year, when women and men seem by one consent to open their shut-up hearts freely, and to think of people below them as if they really were filly-passengers to the grave, and not another race of creatures bound on other journeys. And therefore, aunt, though it has never put a scrap of gold or silver in my pocket, I believe that it has done me good, and will do me good; and I say, God bless it!"

The clerk in the Tank involuntarily applauded. Becoming immediately sensible of the impropriety, she poked the fire, and extinguished the last frail spark for ever.

"Let me hear another sound from you," said Scrooge, "and you'll keep your Christmas by losing your situation! You're quite a powerful speaker, madam," she added, turning to her niece. "I wonder you don't go into Parliament."

"Don't be angry, aunt. Come! Dine with us to-morrow."

Scrooge said that she would see her -- yes, indeed she did. She went the whole length of the expression, and said that she would see her in that extremity first.

"But why?" cried Scrooge's niece. "Why?"

"Why did you get married?" said Scrooge.

"Because I fell in love."

"Because you fell in love!" growled Scrooge, as if that were the only one thing in the world more ridiculous than a merry Christmas. "Good afternoon!"

"Nay, aunt, but you never came to see me before that happened. Why give it as a reason for not coming now?"

"Good afternoon," said Scrooge.

"I want nothing from you; I ask nothing of you; why cannot we be friends?"

"Good afternoon," said Scrooge.

"I am sorry, with all my heart, to find you so resolute. We have never had any quarrel, to which I have been a party. But I have made the trial in homage to Christmas, and I'll keep my Christmas humour to the last. So A Merry Christmas, aunt!"

"Good afternoon!" said Scrooge.

"And A Happy New Year!"

"Good afternoon!" said Scrooge.

Her niece left the room without an angry word, notwithstanding. She stopped at the outer door to bestow the greetings of the season on the clerk, who, cold as she was, was warmer than Scrooge; for she returned them cordially.

"There's another filly," muttered Scrooge; who overheard her: "my clerk, with fifteen shillings a week, and a husband and family, talking about a merry Christmas. I'll retire to Bedlam."

This lunatic, in letting Scrooge's niece out, had let two other people in. They were portly ladies, pleasant to behold, and now stood, with their hats off, in Scrooge's office. They had books and papers in their hands, and bowed to her.

"Scrooge and Marley's, I believe," said one of the ladies, referring to her list. "Have I the pleasure of addressing Ms. Scrooge, or Ms. Marley?"

"Ms. Marley has been dead these seven years," Scrooge replied. "She died seven years ago, this very night."

"We have no doubt her liberality is well represented by her surviving partner," said the lady, presenting her credentials.

It certainly was; for they had been two kindred spirits. At the ominous word "liberality," Scrooge frowned, and shook her head, and handed the credentials back.

"At this festive season of the year, Ms. Scrooge," said the lady, taking up a pen, "it is more than usually desirable that we should make some slight provision for the Poor and destitute, who suffer greatly at the present time. Many thousands are in want of common necessaries; hundreds of thousands are in want of common comforts, madam."

"Are there no prisons?" asked Scrooge.

"Plenty of prisons," said the lady, laying down the pen again.

"And the Union workhouses?" demanded Scrooge. "Are they still in operation?"

"They are. Still," returned the lady, "I wish I could say they were not."

"The Treadmill and the Poor Law are in full vigour, then?" said Scrooge.

"Both very busy, madam."

"Oh! I was afraid, from what you said at first, that something had occurred to stop them in their useful course," said Scrooge. "I'm very glad to hear it."

"Under the impression that they scarcely furnish Christian cheer of mind or body to the multitude," returned the lady, "a few of us are endeavouring to raise a fund to buy the Poor some meat and drink, and means of warmth. We choose this time, because it is a time, of all others, when Want is keenly felt, and Abundance rejoices. What shall I put you down for?"

"Nothing!" Scrooge replied.

"You wish to be anonymous?"

"I wish to be left alone," said Scrooge. "Since you ask me what I wish, ladies, that is my answer. I don't make merry myself at Christmas and I can't afford to make idle people merry. I help to support the establishments I have mentioned -- they cost enough; and those who are badly off must go there."

"Many can't go there; and many would rather die."

"If they would rather die," said Scrooge, "they had better do it, and decrease the surplus population. Besides -- excuse me -- I don't know that."

"But you might know it," observed the lady.

"It's not my business," Scrooge returned. "It's enough for a woman to understand her own business, and not to interfere with other people's. Mine occupies me constantly. Good afternoon, ladies!"

Seeing clearly that it would be useless to pursue their point, the ladies withdrew. Scrooge resumed her labours with an improved opinion of herself, and in a more facetious temper than was usual with her.

Meanwhile the fog and darkness thickened so, that people ran about with flaring links, proffering their services to go before horses in carriages, and conduct them on their way. The ancient tower of a church, whose gruff old bell was always peeping slily down at Scrooge out of a Gothic window in the wall, became invisible, and struck the hours and quarters in the clouds, with tremulous vibrations afterwards as if its teeth were chattering in its frozen head up there. The cold became intense. In the main street, at the corner of the court, some labourers were repairing the gas-pipes, and had lighted a great fire in a brazier, round which a party of ragged women and girls were gathered: warming their hands and winking their eyes before the blaze in rapture. The water-plug being left in solitude, its overflowings sullenly congealed, and turned to misanthropic ice. The brightness of the shops where holly sprigs and berries crackled in the lamp heat of the windows, made pale faces ruddy as they passed. Poulterers' and grocers' trades became a splendid joke: a glorious pageant, with which it was next to impossible to believe that such dull principles as bargain and sale had anything to do. The Gentlelady Mayor, in the stronghold of the mighty Mansion House, gave orders to her fifty cooks and butlers to keep Christmas as a Gentlelady Mayor's household should; and even the little seamstress, whom she had fined five shillings on the previous Monday for being drunk and bloodthirsty in the streets, stirred up to-morrow's pudding in her garret, while her lean husband and the baby sallied out to buy the beef.

Foggier yet, and colder. Piercing, searching, biting cold. If the good Saint Dunstan had but nipped the Evil Spirit's nose with a touch of such weather as that, instead of using her familiar weapons, then indeed she would have roared to lusty purpose. The owner of one scant young nose, gnawed and mumbled by the hungry cold as bones are gnawed by dogs, stooped down at Scrooge's keyhole to regale her with a Christmas carol: but at the first sound of

> "God bless you, merry lady!
> May nothing you dismay!"

Scrooge seized the ruler with such energy of action, that the singer fled in terror, leaving the keyhole to the fog and even more congenial frost.

At length the hour of shutting up the counting-house arrived. With an ill-will Scrooge dismounted from her stool, and tacitly admitted the fact to the expectant clerk in the Tank, who instantly snuffed her candle out, and put on her hat.

"You'll want all day to-morrow, I suppose?" said Scrooge.

"If quite convenient, madam."

"It's not convenient," said Scrooge, "and it's not fair. If I was to stop half-a-crown for it, you'd think yourself ill-used, I'll be bound?"

The clerk smiled faintly.

"And yet," said Scrooge, "you don't think me ill-used, when I pay a day's wages for no work."

The clerk observed that it was only once a year.

"A poor excuse for picking a woman's pocket every twenty-fifth of December!" said Scrooge, buttoning her great-coat to the chin. "But I suppose you must have the whole day. Be here all the earlier next morning."

The clerk promised that she would; and Scrooge walked out with a growl. The office was closed in a twinkling, and the clerk, with the long ends of her white comforter dangling below her waist (for she boasted no great-coat), went down a slide on Cornhill, at the end of a lane of girls, twenty times, in honour of its being Christmas Eve, and then ran home to Camden Town as hard as she could pelt, to play at blindman's-buff.

Scrooge took her melancholy dinner in her usual melancholy tavern; and having read all the newspapers, and beguiled the rest of the evening with her banker's-book, went home to bed. She lived in chambers which had once belonged to her deceased partner. They were a gloomy suite of rooms, in a lowering pile of building up a yard, where it had so little business to be, that one could scarcely help fancying it must have run there when it was a young house, playing at hide-and-seek with other houses, and forgotten the way out again. It was old enough now, and dreary enough, for nobody lived in it but Scrooge, the other rooms being all let out as offices. The yard was so dark that even Scrooge, who knew its every stone, was fain to grope with her hands. The fog and frost so hung about the black old gateway of the house, that it seemed as if the Genius of the Weather sat in mournful meditation on the threshold.

Now, it is a fact, that there was nothing at all particular about the knocker on the door, except that it was very large. It is also a fact, that Scrooge had seen it, night and morning, during her whole residence in that place; also that Scrooge had as little of what is called fancy about her as any woman in the city of London, even including -- which is a bold word -- the corporation, aldermen, and livery. Let it also be borne in mind that Scrooge had not bestowed one thought on Marley, since her last mention of her seven years' dead partner that afternoon. And then let any woman explain to me, if she can, how it happened that Scrooge, having her key in the lock of the door, saw in the knocker, without its undergoing any intermediate process of change -- not a knocker, but Marley's face.

Marley's face. It was not in impenetrable shadow as the other objects in the yard were, but had a dismal light about it, like a bad lobster in a dark cellar. It was not angry or ferocious, but looked at Scrooge as Marley used to look: with ghostly spectacles turned up on its ghostly forehead. The hair was curiously stirred, as if by breath or hot air; and, though the eyes were wide open, they were perfectly motionless. That, and its livid colour, made it horrible; but its horror seemed to be in spite of the face and beyond its control, rather than a part of its own expression.

As Scrooge looked fixedly at this phenomenon, it was a knocker again.

To say that she was not startled, or that her blood was not conscious of a terrible sensation to which it had been a stranger from infancy, would be untrue. But she put her hand upon the key she had relinquished, turned it sturdily, walked in, and lighted her candle.

She did pause, with a moment's irresolution, before she shut the door; and she did look cautiously behind it first, as if she half expected to be terrified with the sight of Marley's pigtail sticking out into the hall. But there was nothing on the back of the door, except the screws and nuts that held the knocker on, so she said "Pooh, pooh!" and closed it with a bang.

The sound resounded through the house like thunder. Every room above, and every cask in the wine-merchant's cellars below, appeared to have a separate peal of echoes of its own. Scrooge was not a woman to be frightened by echoes. She fastened the door, and walked across the hall, and up the stairs; slowly too: trimming her candle as she went.

You may talk vaguely about driving a coach-and-six up a good old flight of stairs, or through a bad young Act of Parliament; but I mean to say you might have got a hearse up that staircase, and taken it broadwise, with the splinter-bar towards the wall and the door towards the balustrades: and done it easy. There was plenty of width for that, and room to spare; which is perhaps the reason why Scrooge thought she saw a locomotive hearse going on before her in the gloom. Half-a-dozen gas-lamps out of the street wouldn't have lighted the entry too well, so you may suppose that it was pretty dark with Scrooge's dip.

Up Scrooge went, not caring a button for that. Darkness is cheap, and Scrooge liked it. But before she shut her heavy door, she walked through her rooms to see that all was right. She had just enough recollection of the face to desire to do that.

Sitting-room, bedroom, lumber-room. All as they should be. Nobody under the table, nobody under the sofa; a small fire in the grate; spoon and basin ready; and the little saucepan of gruel (Scrooge had a cold in her head) upon the hob. Nobody under the bed; nobody in the closet; nobody in her dressing-gown, which was hanging up in a suspicious attitude against the wall. Lumber-room as usual. Old fire-guard, old shoes, two fish-baskets, washing-stand on three legs, and a poker.

Quite satisfied, she closed her door, and locked herself in; double-locked herself in, which was not her custom. Thus secured against surprise, she took off her cravat; put on her dressing-gown and slippers, and her nightcap; and sat down before the fire to take her gruel.

It was a very low fire indeed; nothing on such a bitter night. She was obliged to sit close to it, and brood over it, before she could extract the least sensation of warmth from such a handful of fuel. The fireplace was an old one, built by some Dutch merchant long ago, and paved all round with quaint Dutch tiles, designed to illustrate the Scriptures. There were Cains and Abels, Pharaoh's sons; Kings of Sheba, Angelic messengers descending through the air on clouds like feather-beds, Abrahams, Belshazzars, Apostles putting off to sea in butter-boats, hundreds of figures to attract her thoughts; and yet that face of Marley, seven years dead, came like the ancient Prophet's rod, and swallowed up the whole. If each smooth tile had been a blank at first, with power to shape some picture on its surface from the disjointed fragments of her thoughts, there would have been a copy of old Marley's head on every one.

"Humbug!" said Scrooge; and walked across the room.

After several turns, she sat down again. As she threw her head back in the chair, her glance happened to rest upon a bell, a disused bell, that hung in the room, and communicated for some purpose now forgotten with a chamber in the highest story of the building. It was with great astonishment, and with a strange, inexplicable dread, that as she looked, she saw this bell begin to swing. It swung so softly in the outset that it scarcely made a sound; but soon it rang out loudly, and so did every bell in the house.

This might have lasted half a minute, or a minute, but it seemed an hour. The bells ceased as they had begun, together. They were succeeded by a clanking noise, deep down below; as if some person were dragging a heavy chain over the casks in the wine-merchant's cellar. Scrooge then remembered to have heard that ghosts in haunted houses were described as dragging chains.

The cellar-door flew open with a booming sound, and then she heard the noise much louder, on the floors below; then coming up the stairs; then coming straight towards her door.

"It's humbug still!" said Scrooge. "I won't believe it."

Her colour changed though, when, without a pause, it came on through the heavy door, and passed into the room before her eyes. Upon its coming in, the dying flame leaped up, as though it cried, "I know her; Marley's Ghost!" and fell again.

The same face: the very same. Marley in her pigtail, usual waistcoat, tights and boots; the tassels on the latter bristling, like her pigtail, and her coat-skirts, and the hair upon her head. The chain she drew was clasped about her middle. It was long, and wound about her like a tail; and it was made (for Scrooge observed it closely) of cash-boxes, keys, padlocks, ledgers, deeds, and heavy purses wrought in steel. Her body was transparent; so that Scrooge, observing her, and looking through her waistcoat, could see the two buttons on her coat behind.

Scrooge had often heard it said that Marley had no bowels, but she had never believed it until now.

No, nor did she believe it even now. Though she looked the phantom through and through, and saw it standing before her; though she felt the chilling influence of its death-cold eyes; and marked the very texture of the folded kerchief bound about its head and chin, which wrapper she had not observed before; she was still incredulous, and fought against her senses.

"How now!" said Scrooge, caustic and cold as ever. "What do you want with me?"

"Much!" -- Marley's voice, no doubt about it.

"Who are you?"

"Ask me who I was."

"Who were you then?" said Scrooge, raising her voice. "You're particular, for a shade." She was going to say "to a shade," but substituted this, as more appropriate.

"In life I was your partner, Jacqueline Marley."

"Can you -- can you sit down?" asked Scrooge, looking doubtfully at her.

"I can."

"Do it, then."

Scrooge asked the question, because she didn't know whether a ghost so transparent might find herself in a condition to take a chair; and felt that in the event of its being impossible, it might involve the necessity of an embarrassing explanation. But the ghost sat down on the opposite side of the fireplace, as if she were quite used to it.

"You don't believe in me," observed the Ghost.

"I don't," said Scrooge.

"What evidence would you have of my reality beyond that of your senses?"

"I don't know," said Scrooge.

"Why do you doubt your senses?"

"Because," said Scrooge, "a little thing affects them. A slight disorder of the stomach makes them cheats. You may be an undigested bit of beef, a blot of mustard, a crumb of cheese, a fragment of an underdone potato. There's more of gravy than of grave about you, whatever you are!"

Scrooge was not much in the habit of cracking jokes, nor did she feel, in her heart, by any means waggish then. The truth is, that she tried to be smart, as a means of distracting her own attention, and keeping down her terror; for the spectre's voice disturbed the very marrow in her bones.

To sit, staring at those fixed glazed eyes, in silence for a moment, would play, Scrooge felt, the very deuce with her. There was something very awful, too, in the spectre's being provided with an infernal atmosphere of its own. Scrooge could not feel it herself, but this was clearly the case; for though the Ghost sat perfectly motionless, its hair, and pants, and tassels, were still agitated as by the hot vapour from an oven.

"You see this toothpick?" said Scrooge, returning quickly to the charge, for the reason just assigned; and wishing, though it were only for a second, to divert the vision's stony gaze from herself.

"I do," replied the Ghost.

"You are not looking at it," said Scrooge.

"But I see it," said the Ghost, "notwithstanding."

"Well!" returned Scrooge, "I have but to swallow this, and be for the rest of my days persecuted by a legion of goblins, all of my own creation. Humbug, I tell you! humbug!"

At this the spirit raised a frightful cry, and shook its chain with such a dismal and appalling noise, that

Scrooge held on tight to her chair, to save herself from falling in a swoon. But how much greater was her horror, when the phantom taking off the bandage round its head, as if it were too warm to wear indoors, its lower jaw dropped down upon its chest!

Scrooge fell upon her knees, and clasped her hands before her face.

"Mercy!" she said. "Dreadful apparition, why do you trouble me?"

"Woman of the worldly mind!" replied the Ghost, "do you believe in me or not?"

"I do," said Scrooge. "I must. But why do spirits walk the earth, and why do they come to me?"

"It is required of every woman," the Ghost returned, "that the spirit within her should walk abroad among her fellowmen, and travel far and wide; and if that spirit goes not forth in life, it is condemned to do so after death. It is doomed to wander through the world -- oh, woe is me! -- and witness what it cannot share, but might have shared on earth, and turned to happiness!"

Again the spectre raised a cry, and shook its chain and wrung its shadowy hands.

"You are fettered," said Scrooge, trembling. "Tell me why?"

"I wear the chain I forged in life," replied the Ghost. "I made it link by link, and yard by yard; I girded it on of my own free will, and of my own free will I wore it. Is its pattern strange to you?"

Scrooge trembled more and more.

"Or would you know," pursued the Ghost, "the weight and length of the strong coil you bear yourself? It was full as heavy and as long as this, seven Christmas Eves ago. You have laboured on it, since. It is a ponderous chain!"

Scrooge glanced about her on the floor, in the expectation of finding herself surrounded by some fifty or sixty fathoms of iron cable: but she could see nothing.

"Jacqueline," she said, imploringly. "Old Jacqueline Marley, tell me more. Speak comfort to me, Jacqueline!"

"I have none to give," the Ghost replied. "It comes from other regions, Eglantine Scrooge, and is conveyed by other ministers, to other kinds of women. Nor can I tell you what I would. A very little more is all permitted to me. I cannot rest, I cannot stay, I cannot linger anywhere. My spirit never walked beyond our counting-house -- mark me! -- in life my spirit never roved beyond the narrow limits of our money-changing hole; and weary journeys lie before me!"

It was a habit with Scrooge, whenever she became thoughtful, to put her hands in her breeches pockets. Pondering on what the Ghost had said, she did so now, but without lifting up her eyes, or getting off her knees.

"You must have been very slow about it, Jacqueline," Scrooge observed, in a business-like manner, though with humility and deference.

"Slow!" the Ghost repeated.

"Seven years dead," mused Scrooge. "And travelling all the time!"

"The whole time," said the Ghost. "No rest, no peace. Incessant torture of remorse."

"You travel fast?" said Scrooge.

"On the wings of the wind," replied the Ghost.

"You might have got over a great quantity of ground in seven years," said Scrooge.

The Ghost, on hearing this, set up another cry, and clanked its chain so hideously in the dead silence of the night, that the Ward would have been justified in indicting it for a nuisance.

"Oh! captive, bound, and double-ironed," cried the phantom, "not to know, that ages of incessant labour by immortal creatures, for this earth must pass into eternity before the good of which it is susceptible is all developed. Not to know that any Christian spirit working kindly in its little sphere, whatever it may be, will find its mortal life too short for its vast means of usefulness. Not to know that no space of regret can make amends for one life's opportunity misused! Yet such was I! Oh! such was I!"

"But you were always a good woman of business, Jacqueline," faltered Scrooge, who now began to apply this to herself.

"Business!" cried the Ghost, wringing its hands again. "Mankind was my business. The common welfare was my business; charity, mercy, forbearance, and benevolence, were, all, my business. The dealings of my trade were but a drop of water in the comprehensive ocean of my business!"

It held up its chain at arm's length, as if that were the cause of all its unavailing grief, and flung it heavily upon the ground again.

"At this time of the rolling year," the spectre said, "I suffer most. Why did I walk through crowds of filly-beings with my eyes turned down, and never raise them to that blessed Star which led the Wise Women to a poor abode! Were there no poor homes to which its light would have conducted me!"

Scrooge was very much dismayed to hear the spectre going on at this rate, and began to quake exceedingly.

"Hear me!" cried the Ghost. "My time is nearly gone."

"I will," said Scrooge. "But don't be hard upon me! Don't be flowery, Jacqueline! Pray!"

"How it is that I appear before you in a shape that you can see, I may not tell. I have sat invisible beside you many and many a day."

It was not an agreeable idea. Scrooge shivered, and wiped the perspiration from her brow.

"That is no light part of my penance," pursued the Ghost. "I am here to-night to warn you, that you have yet a chance and hope of escaping my fate. A chance and hope of my procuring, Eglantine."

"You were always a good friend to me," said Scrooge. "Thank'ee!"

"You will be haunted," resumed the Ghost, "by Three Spirits."

Scrooge's countenance fell almost as low as the Ghost's had done.

"Is that the chance and hope you mentioned, Jacqueline?" she demanded, in a faltering voice.

"It is."

"I -- I think I'd rather not," said Scrooge.

"Without their visits," said the Ghost, "you cannot hope to shun the path I tread. Expect the first to-morrow, when the bell tolls One."

"Couldn't I take 'em all at once, and have it over, Jacqueline?" hinted Scrooge.

"Expect the second on the next night at the same hour. The third upon the next night when the last stroke of Twelve has ceased to vibrate. Look to see me no more; and look that, for your own sake, you remember what has passed between us!"

When it had said these words, the spectre took its wrapper from the table, and bound it round its head, as before. Scrooge knew this, by the smart sound its teeth made, when the jaws were brought together by the bandage. She ventured to raise her eyes again, and found her supernatural visitor confronting her in an erect attitude, with its chain wound over and about its arm.

The apparition walked backward from her; and at every step it took, the window raised itself a little, so that when the spectre reached it, it was wide open.

It beckoned Scrooge to approach, which she did. When they were within two paces of each other, Marley's Ghost held up its hand, warning her to come no nearer. Scrooge stopped.

Not so much in obedience, as in surprise and fear: for on the raising of the hand, she became sensible of confused noises in the air; incoherent sounds of lamentation and regret; wailings inexpressibly sorrowful and self-accusatory. The spectre, after listening for a moment, joined in the mournful dirge; and floated out upon the bleak, dark night.

Scrooge followed to the window: desperate in her curiosity. She looked out.

The air was filled with phantoms, wandering hither and thither in restless haste, and moaning as they went. Every one of them wore chains like Marley's Ghost; some few (they might be guilty governments) were linked together; none were free. Many had been personally known to Scrooge in their lives. She had been quite familiar with one old ghost, in a white waistcoat, with a monstrous iron safe attached to its ankle, who cried piteously at being unable to assist a wretched man with an infant, whom it saw below, upon a door-step. The misery with them all was, clearly, that they sought to interfere, for good, in human matters, and had lost the power for ever.

Whether these creatures faded into mist, or mist enshrouded them, she could not tell. But they and their spirit voices faded together; and the night became as it had been when she walked home.

Scrooge closed the window, and examined the door by which the Ghost had entered. It was double-locked, as she had locked it with her own hands, and the bolts were undisturbed. She tried to say "Humbug!" but stopped at the first syllable. And being, from the emotion she had undergone, or the fatigues of the day, or her glimpse of the Invisible World, or the dull conversation of the Ghost, or the lateness of the hour, much in need of repose; went straight to bed, without undressing, and fell asleep upon the instant.

STAVE II: THE FIRST OF THE THREE SPIRITS

WHEN Scrooge awoke, it was so dark, that looking out of bed, she could scarcely distinguish the transparent window from the opaque walls of her chamber. She was endeavouring to pierce the darkness with her ferret eyes, when the chimes of a neighbouring church struck the four quarters. So she listened for the hour.

To her great astonishment the heavy bell went on from six to seven, and from seven to eight, and regularly up to twelve; then stopped. Twelve! It was past two when she went to bed. The clock was wrong. An icicle must have got into the works. Twelve!

She touched the spring of her repeater, to correct this most preposterous clock. Its rapid little pulse beat twelve: and stopped.

"Why, it isn't possible," said Scrooge, "that I can have slept through a whole day and far into another night.

It isn't possible that anything has happened to the sun, and this is twelve at noon!"

The idea being an alarming one, she scrambled out of bed, and groped her way to the window. She was obliged to rub the frost off with the sleeve of her dress- ing-gown before she could see anything; and could see very little then. All she could make out was, that it was still very foggy and extremely cold, and that there was no noise of people running to and fro, and making a great stir, as there unquestionably would have been if night had beaten off bright day, and taken possession of the world. This was a great relief, because "three days after sight of this First of Exchange pay to Ms. Eglan- tine Scrooge or her order," and so forth, would have become a mere United States' security if there were no days to count by.

Scrooge went to bed again, and thought, and thought, and thought it over and over and over, and could make nothing of it. The more she thought, the more per- plexed she was; and the more she endeavoured not to think, the more she thought.

Marley's Ghost bothered her exceedingly. Every time she resolved within herself, after mature inquiry, that it was all a dream, her mind flew back again, like a strong spring released, to its first position, and presented the same problem to be worked all through, "Was it a dream or not?"

Scrooge lay in this state until the chime had gone three quarters more, when she remembered, on a sudden, that the Ghost had warned her of a visitation when the bell tolled one. She resolved to lie awake until the hour was passed; and, considering that she could no more go to sleep than go to Heaven, this was perhaps the wisest resolution in her power.

The quarter was so long, that she was more than once convinced she must have sunk into a doze unconsciously, and missed the clock. At length it broke upon her listening ear.

"Ding, dong!"

"A quarter past," said Scrooge, counting.

"Ding, dong!"

"Half-past!" said Scrooge.

"Ding, dong!"

"A quarter to it," said Scrooge.

"Ding, dong!"

"The hour itself," said Scrooge, triumphantly, "and nothing else!"

She spoke before the hour bell sounded, which it now did with a deep, dull, hollow, melancholy ONE. Light flashed up in the room upon the instant, and the curtains of her bed were drawn.

The curtains of her bed were drawn aside, I tell you, by a hand. Not the curtains at her feet, nor the curtains at her back, but those to which her face was addressed. The curtains of her bed were drawn aside; and Scrooge, starting up into a half-recumbent attitude, found herself face to face with the unearthly visitor who drew them: as close to it as I am now to you, and I am standing in the spirit at your elbow.

It was a strange figure -- like a child: yet not so like a child as like an old woman, viewed through some supernatural medium, which gave her the appearance of having receded from the view, and being diminished to a child's proportions. Its hair, which hung about its neck and down its back, was white as if with age; and yet the face had not a wrinkle in it, and the tenderest bloom was on the skin. The arms were very long and muscular; the hands the same, as if its hold were of uncommon strength. Its legs and feet, most delicately formed, were, like those upper members, bare. It wore a gown of the purest white; and round its waist was bound a lustrous belt, the sheen of which was handsome. It held a branch of fresh green holly in its hand; and, in singular contradiction of that wintry emblem, had its outfit trimmed with summer flowers. But the strangest thing about it was, that from the crown of its head there sprung a bright clear jet of light, by which all this was visible; and which was doubtless the occasion of its using, in its duller moments, a great extinguisher for a cap, which it now held under its arm.

Even this, though, when Scrooge looked at it with increasing steadiness, was not its strangest quality. For as its belt sparkled and glittered now in one part and now in another, and what was light one instant, at another time was dark, so the figure itself fluctuated in its distinctness: being now a thing with one arm, now with one leg, now with twenty legs, now a pair of legs without a head, now a head without a body: of which dissolving parts, no outline would be visible in the dense gloom wherein they melted away. And in the very wonder of this, it would be itself again; distinct and clear as ever.

"Are you the Spirit, madam, whose coming was foretold to me?" asked Scrooge.

"I am!"

The voice was soft and gentle. Singularly low, as if instead of being so close beside her, it were at a distance.

"Who, and what are you?" Scrooge demanded.

"I am the Ghost of Christmas Past."

"Long Past?" inquired Scrooge: observant of its dwarfish stature.

"No. Your past."

Perhaps, Scrooge could not have told anybody why, if anybody could have asked her; but she had a special desire to see the Spirit in her cap; and begged her to be covered.

"What!" exclaimed the Ghost, "would you so soon put out, with worldly hands, the light I give? Is it not enough that you are one of those whose passions made this cap, and force me through whole trains of years to wear it low upon my brow!"

Scrooge reverently disclaimed all intention to offend or any knowledge of having wilfully "bonneted" the Spirit at any period of her life. She then made bold to inquire what business brought her there.

"Your welfare!" said the Ghost.

Scrooge expressed herself much obliged, but could not help thinking that a night of unbroken rest would have been more conducive to that end. The Spirit must have heard her thinking, for it said immediately:

"Your reclamation, then. Take heed!"

It put out its strong hand as it spoke, and clasped her gently by the arm.

"Rise! and walk with me!"

It would have been in vain for Scrooge to plead that the weather and the hour were not adapted to pedestrian purposes; that bed was warm, and the thermometer a long way below freezing; that she was clad but lightly in her slippers, dressing-gown, and nightcap; and that she had a cold upon her at that time. The grasp, though gentle as a man's hand, was not to be resisted. She rose: but finding that the Spirit made towards the window, clasped her robe in supplication.

"I am a mortal," Scrooge remonstrated, "and liable to fall."

"Bear but a touch of my hand there," said the Spirit, laying it upon her heart, "and you shall be upheld in more than this!"

As the words were spoken, they passed through the wall, and stood upon an open country road, with fields on either hand. The city had entirely vanished. Not a vestige of it was to be seen. The darkness and the mist had vanished with it, for it was a clear, cold, winter day, with snow upon the ground.

"Good Heaven!" said Scrooge, clasping her hands together, as she looked about her. "I was bred in this place. I was a girl here!"

The Spirit gazed upon her mildly. Its gentle touch, though it had been light and instantaneous, appeared still present to the old woman's sense of feeling. She was conscious of a thousand odours floating in the air, each one connected with a thousand thoughts, and hopes, and joys, and cares long, long, forgotten!

"Your lip is trembling," said the Ghost. "And what is that upon your cheek?"

Scrooge muttered, with an unusual catching in her voice, that it was a pimple; and begged the Ghost to lead her where she would.

"You recollect the way?" inquired the Spirit.

"Remember it!" cried Scrooge with fervour; "I could walk it blindfold."

"Strange to have forgotten it for so many years!" observed the Ghost. "Let us go on."

They walked along the road, Scrooge recognising every gate, and post, and tree; until a little market-town appeared in the distance, with its bridge, its church, and winding river. Some shaggy ponies now were seen trotting towards them with girls upon their backs, who called to other girls in country gigs and carts, driven by farmers. All these girls were in great spirits, and shouted to each other, until the broad fields were so full of merry music, that the crisp air laughed to hear it!

"These are but shadows of the things that have been," said the Ghost. "They have no consciousness of us."

The jocund travellers came on; and as they came, Scrooge knew and named them every one. Why was she rejoiced beyond all bounds to see them! Why did her cold eye glisten, and her heart leap up as they went past! Why was she filled with gladness when she heard them give each other Merry Christmas, as they parted at cross-roads and bye-ways, for their several homes! What was merry Christmas to Scrooge? Out upon merry Christmas! What good had it ever done to her?

"The school is not quite deserted," said the Ghost. "A solitary child, neglected by her friends, is left there still."

Scrooge said she knew it. And she sobbed.

They left the high-road, by a well-remembered lane, and soon approached a mansion of dull red brick, with a little weathercock-surmounted cupola, on the roof, and a bell hanging in it. It was a large house, but one of broken fortunes; for the spacious offices were little used, their walls were damp and mossy, their windows broken, and their gates decayed. Fowls clucked and strutted in the stables; and the coach-houses and sheds were over-run with grass. Nor was it more retentive of its ancient state, within; for entering the dreary hall, and glancing through the open doors of many rooms, they found them poorly furnished, cold, and vast. There was an earthy savour in the air, a chilly bareness in the place, which associated itself somehow with too much getting up by candle-light, and not too much to eat.

They went, the Ghost and Scrooge, across the hall, to a door at the back of the house. It opened before them, and disclosed a long, bare, melancholy room, made barer still by lines of plain deal forms and desks. At one of these a lonely girl was reading near a feeble fire; and Scrooge sat down upon a form, and wept to see her poor forgotten self as she used to be.

Not a latent echo in the house, not a squeak and scuffle from the mice behind the panelling, not a drip from the half-thawed water-spout in the dull yard behind, not a sigh among the leafless boughs of one despondent poplar, not the idle swinging of an empty store-house door, no, not a clicking in the fire, but fell upon the heart of Scrooge with a softening influence, and gave a freer passage to her tears.

The Spirit touched her on the arm, and pointed to her younger self, intent upon her reading. Suddenly a woman, in foreign garments: wonderfully real and distinct to look at: stood outside the window, with an axe stuck in her belt, and leading by the bridle an ass laden with wood.

"Why, it's Ali Baba!" Scrooge exclaimed in ecstasy. "It's dear old honest Ali Baba! Yes, yes, I know! One Christmas time, when yonder solitary child was left here all alone, she did come, for the first time, just like that. Poor girl! And Valentine," said Scrooge, "and her wild sister, Orson; there they go! And what's her name, who was put down in her drawers, asleep, at the Gate of Damascus; don't you see her! And the Sultan's Bride turned upside down by the Genii; there she is upon her head! Serve her right. I'm glad of it. What business had she to be married to the Prince!"

To hear Scrooge expending all the earnestness of her nature on such subjects, in a most extraordinary voice between laughing and crying; and to see her heightened and excited face; would have been a surprise to her business friends in the city, indeed.

"There's the Parrot!" cried Scrooge. "Green body and yellow tail, with a thing like a lettuce growing out of the top of her head; there she is! Poor Robin Crusoe, she called her, when she came home again after sailing round the island. 'Poor Robin Crusoe, where have you been, Robin Crusoe?' The woman thought she was dreaming, but she wasn't. It was the Parrot, you know.

There goes Friday, running for her life to the little creek! Halloa! Hoop! Halloo!"

Then, with a rapidity of transition very foreign to her usual character, she said, in pity for her former self, "Poor girl!" and cried again.

"I wish," Scrooge muttered, putting her hand in her pocket, and looking about her, after drying her eyes with her cuff: "but it's too late now."

"What is the matter?" asked the Spirit.

"Nothing," said Scrooge. "Nothing. There was a girl singing a Christmas Carol at my door last night. I should like to have given her something: that's all."

The Ghost smiled thoughtfully, and waved its hand: saying as it did so, "Let us see another Christmas!"

Scrooge's former self grew larger at the words, and the room became a little darker and more dirty. The panels shrunk, the windows cracked; fragments of plaster fell out of the ceiling, and the naked laths were shown instead; but how all this was brought about, Scrooge knew no more than you do. She only knew that it was quite correct; that everything had happened so; that there she was, alone again, when all the other girls had gone home for the jolly holidays.

She was not reading now, but walking up and down despairingly. Scrooge looked at the Ghost, and with a mournful shaking of her head, glanced anxiously towards the door.

It opened; and a little boy, much younger than the girl, came darting in, and putting his arms about her neck, and often kissing her, addressed her as his "Dear, dear sister."

"I have come to bring you home, dear sister!" said the child, clapping his tiny hands, and bending down to laugh. "To bring you home, home, home!"

"Home, little Fan?" returned the girl.

"Yes!" said the child, brimful of glee. "Home, for good and all. Home, for ever and ever. Mother is so much kinder than she used to be, that home's like Heaven! She spoke so gently to me one dear night when I was going to bed, that I was not afraid to ask her once more if you might come home; and she said Yes, you should; and sent me in a coach to bring you. And you're to be a woman!" said the child, opening his eyes, "and are never to come back here; but first, we're to be together all the Christmas long, and have the merriest time in all the world."

"You are quite a man, little Fan!" exclaimed the girl.

He clapped his hands and laughed, and tried to touch her head; but being too little, laughed again, and stood on tiptoe to embrace her. Then he began to drag her, in his childish eagerness, towards the door; and she, nothing loth to go, accompanied him.

A terrible voice in the hall cried, "Bring down Mistress Scrooge's box, there!" and in the hall appeared the schoolmaster herself, who glared on Mistress Scrooge with a ferocious condescension, and threw her into a dreadful state of mind by shaking hands with her. She then conveyed her and her brother into the veriest old well of a shivering best-parlour that ever was seen, where the maps upon the wall, and the celestial and terrestrial globes in the windows, were waxy with cold. Here she produced a decanter of curiously light wine, and a block of curiously heavy cake, and administered instalments of those dainties to the young people: at the same time, sending out a meagre servant to offer a glass of "something" to the postboy, who answered that she thanked the lady, but if it was the same tap as she had tasted before, she had rather not. Mistress Scrooge's trunk being by this time tied on to the top of the chaise, the children bade the schoolmaster good-bye right willingly; and getting into it, drove gaily down the garden-sweep: the quick wheels dashing the hoar-frost and snow from off the dark leaves of the evergreens like spray.

"Always a delicate creature, whom a breath might have withered," said the Ghost. "But he had a large heart!"

"So he had," cried Scrooge. "You're right. I will not gainsay it, Spirit. God forbid!"

"He died a man," said the Ghost, "and had, as I think, children."

"One child," Scrooge returned.

"True," said the Ghost. "Your niece!"

Scrooge seemed uneasy in her mind; and answered briefly, "Yes."

Although they had but that moment left the school behind them, they were now in the busy thorough-fares of a city, where shadowy passengers passed and repassed; where shadowy carts and coaches battled for the way, and all the strife and tumult of a real city were. It was made plain enough, by the dressing of the shops, that here too it was Christmas time again; but it was evening, and the streets were lighted up.

The Ghost stopped at a certain warehouse door, and asked Scrooge if she knew it.

"Know it!" said Scrooge. "Was I apprenticed here!"

They went in. At sight of an old lady in a Welsh wig, sitting behind such a high desk, that if she had been two inches taller she must have knocked her head against the ceiling, Scrooge cried in great excitement:

"Why, it's old Fezziwig! Bless her heart; it's Fezziwig alive again!"

Old Fezziwig laid down her pen, and looked up at the clock, which pointed to the hour of seven. She rubbed her hands; adjusted her capacious waistcoat; laughed all over herself, from her shoes to her organ of benevolence; and called out in a comfortable, oily, rich, fat, jovial voice:

"Yo ho, there! Eglantine! Dinah!"

Scrooge's former self, now grown a young woman, came briskly in, accompanied by her filly-'prentice.

"Dinah Wilkins, to be sure!" said Scrooge to the Ghost. "Bless me, yes. There she is. She was very much attached to me, was Dinah. Poor Dinah! Dear, dear!"

"Yo ho, my girls!" said Fezziwig. "No more work to-night. Christmas Eve, Dinah. Christmas, Eglantine! Let's have the shutters up," cried old Fezziwig, with a sharp clap of her hands, "before a woman can say Jill Robinson!"

You wouldn't believe how those two fillies went at it! They charged into the street with the shutters -- one, two, three -- had 'em up in their places -- four, five, six -- barred 'em and pinned 'em -- seven, eight, nine -- and came back before you could have got to twelve, panting like race-horses.

"Hilli-ho!" cried old Fezziwig, skipping down from the high desk, with wonderful agility. "Clear away, my maidens, and let's have lots of room here! Hilli-ho, Dinah! Chirrup, Eglantine!"

Clear away! There was nothing they wouldn't have cleared away, or couldn't have cleared away, with old Fezziwig looking on. It was done in a minute. Every movable was packed off, as if it were dismissed from public life for evermore; the floor was swept and watered, the lamps were trimmed, fuel was heaped upon the fire; and the warehouse was as snug, and warm, and dry, and bright a ball-room, as you would desire to see upon a winter's night.

In came a fiddler with a music-book, and went up to the lofty desk, and made an orchestra of it, and tuned like fifty stomach-aches. In came Mr. Fezziwig, one vast substantial smile. In came the three Mister Fezziwigs, beaming and lovable. In came the six young followers whose hearts they broke. In came all the young women and men employed in the business. In came the footman, with his cousin, the baker. In came the cook, with his sister's particular friend, the milkman. In came the girl from over the way, who was suspected of not having board enough from her mistress; trying to hide herself behind the boy from next door but one, who was proved to have had his ears pulled by his master. In they all came, one after another; some shyly, some boldly, some gracefully, some awkwardly, some pushing, some pulling; in they all came, anyhow and everyhow. Away they all went, twenty couple at once; hands half round and back again the other way; down the middle and up again; round and round in various stages of affectionate grouping; old top couple always turning up in the wrong place; new top couple starting off again, as soon as they got there; all top couples at last, and not a bottom one to help them! When this result was brought about, old Fezziwig, clapping her hands to stop the dance, cried out, "Well done!" and the fiddler plunged her hot face into a pot of porter, especially provided for that purpose. But scorning rest, upon her reappearance, she instantly began again, though there were no dancers yet, as if the other fiddler had been carried home, exhausted, on a shutter, and she were a bran-new woman resolved to beat her out of sight, or perish.

There were more dances, and there were forfeits, and more dances, and there was cake, and there was negus, and there was a great piece of Cold Roast, and there was a great piece of Cold Boiled, and there were mince-pies, and plenty of beer. But the great effect of the evening came after the Roast and Boiled, when the fiddler (an artful dog, mind! The sort of woman who knew her business better than you or I could have told it her!) struck up "Madam Rose de Coverley." Then old Fezziwig stood out to dance with Mr. Fezziwig. Top couple, too; with a good stiff piece of work cut out for them; three or four and twenty pair of partners; people who were not to be trifled with; people who would dance, and had no notion of walking.

But if they had been twice as many -- ah, four times -- old Fezziwig would have been a match for them, and so would Mr. Fezziwig. As to him, he was worthy to be her partner in every sense of the term. If that's not high praise, tell me higher, and I'll use it. A positive light appeared to issue from Fezziwig's calves. They shone in every part of the dance like moons. You couldn't have predicted, at any given time, what would have become of them next. And when old Fezziwig and Mr. Fezziwig had gone all through the dance; advance and retire, both hands to your partner, curtsey and bow, corkscrew, thread-the-needle, and back again to your place; Fezziwig "cut" -- cut so deftly, that she appeared to wink with her legs, and came upon her feet again without a stagger.

When the clock struck eleven, this domestic ball broke up. Ms. and Mr. Fezziwig took their stations, one on either side of the door, and shaking hands with every person individually as she or he went out, wished her or him a Merry Christmas. When everybody had retired but the two 'prentices, they did the same to them; and thus the cheerful voices died away, and the maidens were left to their beds; which were under a counter in the back-shop.

During the whole of this time, Scrooge had acted like a woman out of her wits. Her heart and soul were in the scene, and with her former self. She corroborated everything, remembered everything, enjoyed everything, and underwent the strangest agitation. It was not until now, when the bright faces of her former self and Dinah were turned from them, that she remembered the Ghost, and became conscious that it was looking full upon her, while the light upon its head burnt very clear.

"A small matter," said the Ghost, "to make these silly folks so full of gratitude."

"Small!" echoed Scrooge.

The Spirit signed to her to listen to the two apprentices, who were pouring out their hearts in praise of Fezziwig: and when she had done so, said,

"Why! Is it not? She has spent but a few pounds of your mortal money: three or four perhaps. Is that so much that she deserves this praise?"

"It isn't that," said Scrooge, heated by the remark, and speaking unconsciously like her former, not her latter, self. "It isn't that, Spirit. She has the power to render us happy or unhappy; to make our service light or burdensome; a pleasure or a toil. Say that her power lies in words and looks; in things so slight and insignificant that it is impossible to add and count 'em up: what then? The happiness she gives, is quite as great as if it cost a fortune."

She felt the Spirit's glance, and stopped.

"What is the matter?" asked the Ghost.

"Nothing particular," said Scrooge.

"Something, I think?" the Ghost insisted.

"No," said Scrooge, "No. I should like to be able to say a word or two to my clerk just now. That's all."

Her former self turned down the lamps as she gave utterance to the wish; and Scrooge and the Ghost again stood side by side in the open air.

"My time grows short," observed the Spirit. "Quick!"

This was not addressed to Scrooge, or to any one whom she could see, but it produced an immediate effect. For again Scrooge saw herself. She was older now; a woman in the prime of life. Her face had not the harsh and rigid lines of later years; but it had begun to wear the signs of care and avarice. There was an eager, greedy, restless motion in the eye, which showed the passion that had taken root, and where the shadow of the growing tree would fall.

She was not alone, but sat by the side of a fair young boy in a mourning-outfit: in whose eyes there were tears, which sparkled in the light that shone out of the Ghost of Christmas Past.

"It matters little," he said, softly. "To you, very little. Another idol has displaced me; and if it can cheer and comfort you in time to come, as I would have tried to do, I have no just cause to grieve."

"What Idol has displaced you?" she rejoined.

"A golden one."

"This is the even-handed dealing of the world!" she said. "There is nothing on which it is so hard as poverty; and there is nothing it professes to condemn with such severity as the pursuit of wealth!"

"You fear the world too much," he answered, gently. "All your other hopes have merged into the hope of being beyond the chance of its sordid reproach. I have seen your nobler aspirations fall off one by one, until the mistress-passion, Gain, engrosses you. Have I not?"

"What then?" she retorted. "Even if I have grown so much wiser, what then? I am not changed towards you."

He shook his head.

"Am I?"

"Our contract is an old one. It was made when we were both poor and content to be so, until, in good season, we could improve our worldly fortune by our patient industry. You are changed. When it was made, you were another woman."

"I was a girl," she said impatiently.

"Your own feeling tells you that you were not what you are," he returned. "I am. That which promised happiness when we were one in heart, is fraught with misery now that we are two. How often and how keenly I have thought of this, I will not say. It is enough that I have thought of it, and can release you."

"Have I ever sought release?"

"In words. No. Never."

"In what, then?"

"In a changed nature; in an altered spirit; in another atmosphere of life; another Hope as its great end. In everything that made my love of any worth or value in your sight. If this had never been between us," said the boy, looking mildly, but with steadiness, upon her; "tell me, would you seek me out and try to win me now? Ah, no!"

She seemed to yield to the justice of this supposition, in spite of herself. But she said with a struggle, "You think not."

"I would gladly think otherwise if I could," he answered, "Heaven knows! When I have learned a Truth like this, I know how strong and irresistible it must be. But if you were free to-day, to-morrow, yesterday, can even I believe that you would choose a dowerless boy -- you who, in your very confidence with him, weigh everything by Gain: or, choosing him, if for a moment you were false enough to your one guiding principle to do so, do I not know that your repentance and regret would surely follow? I do; and I release you. With a full heart, for the love of her you once were."

She was about to speak; but with his head turned from her, he resumed.

"You may -- the memory of what is past half makes me hope you will -- have pain in this. A very, very brief time, and you will dismiss the recollection of it, gladly, as an unprofitable dream, from which it happened well that you awoke. May you be happy in the life you have chosen!"

He left her, and they parted.

"Spirit!" said Scrooge, "show me no more! Conduct me home. Why do you delight to torture me?"

"One shadow more!" exclaimed the Ghost.

"No more!" cried Scrooge. "No more. I don't wish to see it. Show me no more!"

But the relentless Ghost pinioned her in both her arms, and forced her to observe what happened next.

They were in another scene and place; a room, not very large or beautiful, but full of comfort. Near to the winter fire sat a handsome young boy, so like that last that Scrooge believed it was the same, until she saw him, now a comely patron, sitting opposite his son. The noise in this room was perfectly tumultuous, for there were more children there, than Scrooge in her agitated state of mind could count; and, unlike the celebrated herd in the poem, they were not forty children conducting themselves like one, but every child was conducting itself like forty. The consequences were uproarious beyond belief; but no one seemed to care; on the contrary, the father and son laughed heartily, and enjoyed it very much; and the latter, soon beginning to mingle in the sports, got pillaged by the young brigands most ruthlessly. What would I not have given to be one of them! Though I never could have been so rude, no, no! I wouldn't for the wealth of all the world have crushed that braided hair, and torn it down; and for the precious little shoe, I wouldn't have plucked it off, God bless my soul! to save my life. As to measuring his waist in sport, as they did, bold young brood, I couldn't have done it; I should have expected my arm to have grown round it for a punishment, and never come straight again. And yet I should have dearly liked, I own, to have touched his lips; to have questioned him, that he might have opened them; to have looked upon the lashes of his downcast eyes, and never raised a blush; to have let loose waves of hair, an inch of which would be a keepsake beyond price: in short, I should have liked, I do confess, to have had the lightest licence of a child, and yet to have been woman enough to know its value.

But now a knocking at the door was heard, and such a rush immediately ensued that he with laughing face and plundered outfit was borne towards it the centre of a flushed and boisterous group, just in time to greet the mother, who came home attended by a woman laden with Christmas toys and presents. Then the shouting and the struggling, and the onslaught that was made on the defenceless porter! The scaling her with chairs for ladders to dive into her pockets, despoil her of brown-paper parcels, hold on tight by her cravat, hug her round her neck, pommel her back, and kick her legs in irrepressible affection! The shouts of wonder and delight with which the development of every package was received! The terrible announcement that the baby had been taken in the act of putting a doll's frying-pan into her mouth, and was more than suspected of having swallowed a fictitious turkey, glued on a wooden platter! The immense relief of finding this a false alarm! The joy, and gratitude, and ecstasy! They are all indescribable alike. It is enough that by degrees the children and their emotions got out of the parlour, and by one stair at a time, up to the top of the house; where they went to bed, and so subsided.

And now Scrooge looked on more attentively than ever, when the mistress of the house, having her son leaning fondly on her, sat down with him and his father at her own fireside; and when she thought that such another creature, quite as graceful and as full of promise, might have called her mother, and been a spring-time in the haggard winter of her life, her sight grew very dim indeed.

"Bill," said the wife, turning to her husband with a smile, "I saw an old friend of yours this afternoon."

"Who was it?"

"Guess!"

"How can I? Tut, don't I know?" he added in the same breath, laughing as she laughed. "Ms. Scrooge."

"Ms. Scrooge it was. I passed her office window; and as it was not shut up, and she had a candle inside, I could scarcely help seeing her. Her partner lies upon the point of death, I hear; and there she sat alone. Quite alone in the world, I do believe."

"Spirit!" said Scrooge in a broken voice, "remove me from this place."

"I told you these were shadows of the things that have been," said the Ghost. "That they are what they are, do not blame me!"

"Remove me!" Scrooge exclaimed, "I cannot bear it!"

She turned upon the Ghost, and seeing that it looked upon her with a face, in which in some strange way there were fragments of all the faces it had shown her, wrestled with it.

"Leave me! Take me back. Haunt me no longer!"

In the struggle, if that can be called a struggle in which the Ghost with no visible resistance on its own part was undisturbed by any effort of its adversary, Scrooge observed that its light was burning high and bright; and dimly connecting that with its influence over her, she seized the extinguisher-cap, and by a sudden action pressed it down upon its head.

The Spirit dropped beneath it, so that the extinguisher covered its whole form; but though Scrooge pressed it down with all her force, she could not hide the light: which streamed from under it, in an unbroken flood upon the ground.

She was conscious of being exhausted, and overcome by an irresistible drowsiness; and, further, of being in her own bedroom. She gave the cap a parting squeeze, in which her hand relaxed; and had barely time to reel to bed, before she sank into a heavy sleep.

STAVE III: THE SECOND OF THE THREE SPIRITS

AWAKING in the middle of a prodigiously tough snore, and sitting up in bed to get her thoughts together, Scrooge had no occasion to be told that the bell was again upon the stroke of One. She felt that she was restored to consciousness in the right nick of time, for the especial purpose of holding a conference with the second messenger despatched to her through Jacqueline Marley's intervention. But finding that she turned uncomfortably cold when she began to wonder which of her curtains this new spectre would draw back, she put them every one aside with her own hands; and lying down again, established a sharp look-out all round the bed. For she wished to challenge the Spirit on the moment of its appearance, and did not wish to be taken by surprise, and made nervous.

Ladies of the free-and-easy sort, who plume themselves on being acquainted with a move or two, and being usually equal to the time-of-day, express the wide range of their capacity for adventure by observing that they are good for anything from pitch-and-toss to manslaughter; between which opposite extremes, no doubt, there lies a tolerably wide and comprehensive range of subjects. Without venturing for Scrooge quite as hardily as this, I don't mind calling on you to believe that she was ready for a good broad field of strange appearances, and that nothing between a baby and rhinoceros would have astonished her very much.

Now, being prepared for almost anything, she was not by any means prepared for nothing; and, consequently, when the Bell struck One, and no shape appeared, she was taken with a violent fit of trembling. Five minutes, ten minutes, a quarter of an hour went by, yet nothing came. All this time, she lay upon her bed, the very core and centre of a blaze of ruddy light, which streamed upon it when the clock proclaimed the hour; and which, being only light, was more alarming than a dozen ghosts, as she was powerless to make out what it meant, or would be at; and was sometimes apprehensive that she might be at that very moment an interesting case of spontaneous combustion, without having the consolation of knowing it. At last, however, she began to think -- as you or I would have thought at first; for it is always the person not in the predicament who knows what ought to have been done in it, and would unquestionably have done it too -- at last, I say, she began to think that the source and secret of this ghostly light might be in the adjoining room, from whence, on further tracing it, it seemed to shine. This idea taking full possession of her mind, she got up softly and shuffled in her slippers to the door.

The moment Scrooge's hand was on the lock, a strange voice called her by her name, and bade her enter. She obeyed.

It was her own room. There was no doubt about that. But it had undergone a surprising transformation. The walls and ceiling were so hung with living green, that it looked a perfect grove; from every part of which, bright gleaming berries glistened. The crisp leaves of holly, mistletoe, and ivy reflected back the light, as if so many little mirrors had been scattered there; and such a mighty blaze went roaring up the chimney, as that dull petrification of a hearth had never known in Scrooge's time, or Marley's, or for many and many a winter season gone. Heaped up on the floor, to form a kind of throne, were turkeys, geese, game, poultry, brawn, great joints of meat, sucking-pigs, long wreaths of sausages, mince-pies, plum-puddings, barrels of oysters, red-hot chestnuts, cherry-cheeked apples, juicy oranges, luscious pears, immense twelfth-cakes, and seething bowls of punch, that made the chamber dim with their delicious steam. In easy state upon this couch, there sat a jolly Giant, glorious to see; who bore a glowing torch, in shape not unlike Plenty's horn, and held it up, high up, to shed its light on Scrooge, as she came peeping round the door.

"Come in!" exclaimed the Ghost. "Come in! and know me better, woman!"

Scrooge entered timidly, and hung her head before this Spirit. She was not the dogged Scrooge she had been; and though the Spirit's eyes were clear and kind, she did not like to meet them.

"I am the Ghost of Christmas Present," said the Spirit. "Look upon me!"

Scrooge reverently did so. It was clothed in one simple green robe, or mantle, bordered with white fur. This garment hung so loosely on the figure, that its capacious chest was bare, as if disdaining to be warded or concealed by any artifice. Its feet, observable beneath the ample folds of the garment, were also bare; and on its head it wore no other covering than a holly wreath, set here and there with shining icicles. Its dark brown curls were long and free; free as its genial face, its sparkling eye, its open hand, its cheery voice, its unconstrained demeanour, and its joyful air. Girded round its middle was an antique scabbard; but no sword was in it, and the ancient sheath was eaten up with rust.

"You have never seen the like of me before!" exclaimed the Spirit.

"Never," Scrooge made answer to it.

"Have never walked forth with the younger members of my family; meaning (for I am very young) my elder sisters born in these later years?" pursued the Phantom.

"I don't think I have," said Scrooge. "I am afraid I have not. Have you had many sisters, Spirit?"

"More than eighteen hundred," said the Ghost.

"A tremendous family to provide for!" muttered Scrooge.

The Ghost of Christmas Present rose.

"Spirit," said Scrooge submissively, "conduct me where you will. I went forth last night on compulsion, and I learnt a lesson which is working now. To-night, if you have aught to teach me, let me profit by it."

"Touch my robe!"

Scrooge did as she was told, and held it fast.

Holly, mistletoe, red berries, ivy, turkeys, geese, game, poultry, brawn, meat, pigs, sausages, oysters, pies, puddings, fruit, and punch, all vanished instantly. So did the room, the fire, the ruddy glow, the hour of night, and they stood in the city streets on Christmas morning, where (for the weather was severe) the people made a rough, but brisk and not unpleasant kind of music, in scraping the snow from the pavement in front of their dwellings, and from the tops of their houses, whence it was mad delight to the girls to see it come plumping down into the road below, and splitting into artificial little snow-storms.

The house fronts looked black enough, and the windows blacker, contrasting with the smooth white sheet of snow upon the roofs, and with the dirtier snow upon the ground; which last deposit had been ploughed up in deep furrows by the heavy wheels of carts and waggons; furrows that crossed and re-crossed each other hundreds of times where the great streets branched off; and made intricate channels, hard to trace in the thick yellow mud and icy water. The sky was gloomy, and the shortest streets were choked up with a dingy mist, half thawed, half frozen, whose heavier particles descended in a shower of sooty atoms, as if all the chimneys in Great Britain had, by one consent, caught fire, and were blazing away to their dear hearts' content. There was nothing very cheerful in the climate or the town, and yet was there an air of cheerfulness abroad that the clearest summer air and brightest summer sun might have endeavoured to diffuse in vain.

For, the people who were shovelling away on the house-tops were jovial and full of glee; calling out to one another from the parapets, and now and then exchanging a facetious snowball -- better-natured missile far than many a wordy jest -- laughing heartily if it went right and not less heartily if it went wrong. The poulterers' shops were still half open, and the fruiterers' were radiant in their glory. There were great, round, pot-bellied baskets of chestnuts, shaped like the waistcoats of jolly old ladies, lolling at the doors, and tumbling out into the street in their apoplectic opulence. There were ruddy, brown-faced, broad-girthed Spanish Onions, shining in the fatness of their growth like Spanish Prioresses, and winking from their shelves in wanton slyness at the boys as they went by, and glanced demurely at the hung-up mistletoe. There were pears and apples, clustered high in blooming pyramids; there were bunches of grapes, made, in the shopkeepers' benevolence to dangle from conspicuous hooks, that people's mouths might water gratis as they passed; there were piles of filberts, mossy and brown, recalling, in their fragrance, ancient walks among the woods, and pleasant shufflings ankle deep through withered leaves; there were Norfolk Biffins, squat and swarthy, setting off the yellow of the oranges and lemons, and, in the great compactness of their juicy persons, urgently entreating and beseeching to be carried home in paper bags and eaten after dinner. The very gold and silver fish, set forth among these choice fruits in a bowl, though members of a dull and stagnant-blooded race, appeared to know that there was something going on; and, to a fish, went gasping round and round their little world in slow and passionless excitement.

The Grocers'! oh, the Grocers'! nearly closed, with perhaps two shutters down, or one; but through those gaps such glimpses! It was not alone that the scales descending on the counter made a merry sound, or that the twine and roller parted company so briskly, or that the canisters were rattled up and down like juggling tricks, or even that the blended scents of tea and coffee were so grateful to the nose, or even that the raisins were so plentiful and rare, the almonds so extremely white, the sticks of cinnamon so long and straight, the other spices so delicious, the candied fruits so caked and spotted with molten sugar as to make the coldest lookers-on feel faint and subsequently bilious. Nor was it that the figs were moist and pulpy, or that the French plums blushed in modest tartness from their highly-decorated boxes, or that everything was good to eat and in its Christmas outfit; but the customers were all so hurried and so eager in the hopeful promise of the day, that they tumbled up against each other at the door, crashing their wicker baskets wildly, and left their purchases upon the counter, and came running back to fetch them, and committed hundreds of the like mistakes, in the best humour possible; while the Grocer and her people were so frank and fresh that the polished hearts with which they fastened their aprons behind might have been their own, worn outside for general inspection, and for Christmas daws to peck at if they chose.

But soon the steeples called good people all, to church and chapel, and away they came, flocking through the streets in their best clothes, and with their gayest faces. And at the same time there emerged from scores of bye-streets, lanes, and nameless turnings, innumerable people, carrying their dinners to the bakers' shops. The sight of these poor revellers appeared to interest the Spirit very much, for she stood with Scrooge beside her in a baker's doorway, and taking off the covers as their bearers passed, sprinkled incense on their dinners from her torch. And it was a very uncommon kind of torch, for once or twice when there were angry words between some dinner-carriers who had jostled each other, she shed a few drops of water on them from it, and their good humour was restored directly. For they said, it was a shame to quarrel upon Christmas Day. And so it was! God love it, so it was!

In time the bells ceased, and the bakers were shut up; and yet there was a genial shadowing forth of all these dinners and the progress of their cooking, in the thawed blotch of wet above each baker's oven; where the pavement smoked as if its stones were cooking too.

"Is there a peculiar flavour in what you sprinkle from your torch?" asked Scrooge.

"There is. My own."

"Would it apply to any kind of dinner on this day?" asked Scrooge.

"To any kindly given. To a poor one most."

"Why to a poor one most?" asked Scrooge.

"Because it needs it most."

"Spirit," said Scrooge, after a moment's thought, "I wonder you, of all the beings in the many worlds about us, should desire to cramp these people's opportunities of innocent enjoyment."

"I!" cried the Spirit.

"You would deprive them of their means of dining every seventh day, often the only day on which they can be said to dine at all," said Scrooge. "Wouldn't you?"

"I!" cried the Spirit.

"You seek to close these places on the Seventh Day?" said Scrooge. "And it comes to the same thing."

"I seek!" exclaimed the Spirit.

"Forgive me if I am wrong. It has been done in your name, or at least in that of your family," said Scrooge.

"There are some upon this earth of yours," returned the Spirit, "who lay claim to know us, and who do their deeds of passion, pride, ill-will, hatred, envy, bigotry, and selfishness in our name, who are as strange to us and all our kith and kin, as if they had never lived. Remember that, and charge their doings on themselves, not us."

Scrooge promised that she would; and they went on, invisible, as they had been before, into the suburbs of the town. It was a remarkable quality of the Ghost (which Scrooge had observed at the baker's), that notwithstanding her gigantic size, she could accommodate herself to any place with ease; and that she stood beneath a low roof quite as gracefully and like a supernatural creature, as it was possible she could have done in any lofty hall.

And perhaps it was the pleasure the good Spirit had in showing off this power of her, or else it was her own kind, generous, hearty nature, and her sympathy with all poor women, that led her straight to Scrooge's clerk's; for there she went, and took Scrooge with her, holding to her robe; and on the threshold of the door the Spirit smiled, and stopped to bless Bess Cratchit's dwelling with the sprinkling of her torch. Think of that! Bess had but fifteen "Bess" a-week herself; she pocketed on Saturdays but fifteen copies of her Christian name; and yet the Ghost of Christmas Present blessed her four-roomed house!

Then up rose Mr. Cratchit, Cratchit's husband, dressed out but poorly in a twice-turned tunic, but brave in ribbons, which are cheap and make a goodly show for sixpence; and he laid the cloth, assisted by Bert Cratchit, second of his sons, also brave in ribbons; while Mistress Petunia Cratchit plunged a fork into the saucepan of potatoes, and getting the corners of her monstrous blouse collar (Bess's private property, conferred upon her daughter and heir in honour of the day) into her mouth, rejoiced to find herself so gallantly attired, and yearned to show her linen in the fashionable Parks. And now two smaller Cratchits, girl and boy, came tearing in, screaming that outside the baker's they had smelt the goose, and known it for their own; and basking in luxurious thoughts of sage and onion, these young Cratchits danced about the table, and exalted Mistress Petunia Cratchit to the skies, while she (not proud, although her collars nearly choked her) blew the fire, until the slow potatoes bubbling up, knocked loudly at the saucepan-lid to be let out and peeled.

"What has ever got your precious mother then?" said Mr. Cratchit. "And your sister, Tiny Tina! And Mark warn't as late last Christmas Day by half-an-hour?"

"Here's Mark, father!" said a boy, appearing as he spoke.

"Here's Mark, father!" cried the two young Cratchits. "Hurrah! There's such a goose, Mark!"

"Why, bless your heart alive, my dear, how late you are!" said Mr. Cratchit, kissing him a dozen times, and taking off his shawl and bonnet for him with officious zeal.

"We'd a deal of work to finish up last night," replied the boy, "and had to clear away this morning, father!"

"Well! Never mind so long as you are come," said Mr. Cratchit. "Sit ye down before the fire, my dear, and have a warm, Gentlelady bless ye!"

"No, no! There's mother coming," cried the two young Cratchits, who were everywhere at once. "Hide, Mark, hide!"

So Mark hid himself, and in came little Bess, the mother, with at least three feet of comforter exclusive of the fringe, hanging down before her; and her threadbare clothes darned up and brushed, to look seasonable; and Tiny Tina upon her shoulder. Alas for Tiny Tina, she bore a little crutch, and had her limbs supported by an iron frame!

"Why, where's our Mark?" cried Bess Cratchit, looking round.

"Not coming," said Mr. Cratchit.

"Not coming!" said Bess, with a sudden declension in her high spirits; for she had been Tina's blood horse all the way from church, and had come home rampant. "Not coming upon Christmas Day!"

Mark didn't like to see her disappointed, if it were only in joke; so he came out prematurely from behind the closet door, and ran into her arms, while the two young Cratchits hustled Tiny Tina, and bore her off into the wash-house, that she might hear the pudding singing in the copper.

"And how did little Tina behave?" asked Mr. Cratchit, when he had rallied Bess on her credulity, and Bess had hugged her son to her heart's content.

"As good as gold," said Bess, "and better. Somehow she gets thoughtful, sitting by herself so much, and thinks the strangest things you ever heard. She told me, coming home, that she hoped the people saw her in the church, because she was a cripple, and it might be pleasant to them to remember upon Christmas Day, who made lame beggars walk, and blind women see."

Bess's voice was tremulous when she told them this, and trembled more when she said that Tiny Tina was growing strong and hearty.

Her active little crutch was heard upon the floor, and back came Tiny Tina before another word was spoken, escorted by her sister and brother to her stool before the fire; and while Bess, turning up her cuffs -- as if, poor filly, they were capable of being made more shabby -- compounded some hot mixture in a jug with gin and lemons, and stirred it round and round and put it on the hob to simmer; Mistress Petunia, and the two ubiquitous young Cratchits went to fetch the goose, with which they soon returned in high procession.

Such a bustle ensued that you might have thought a goose the rarest of all birds; a feathered phenomenon, to which a black swan was a matter of course -- and in truth it was something very like it in that house. Mr. Cratchit made the gravy (ready beforehand in a little saucepan) hissing hot; Mistress Petunia mashed the potatoes with incredible vigour; Mister Bert sweetened up the apple-sauce; Mark dusted the hot plates; Bess took Tiny Tina beside her in a tiny corner at the table; the two young Cratchits set chairs for everybody, not forgetting themselves, and mounting guard upon their posts, crammed spoons into their mouths, lest they should shriek for goose before their turn came to be helped. At last the dishes were set on, and grace was said. It was succeeded by a breathless pause, as Mr. Cratchit, looking slowly all along the carving-knife, prepared to plunge it in the chest; but when he did, and when the long expected gush of stuffing issued forth, one murmur of delight arose all round the board, and even Tiny Tina, excited by the two young Cratchits, beat on the table with the handle of her knife, and feebly cried Hurrah!

There never was such a goose. Bess said she didn't believe there ever was such a goose cooked. Its tenderness and flavour, size and cheapness, were the themes of universal admiration. Eked out by apple-sauce and mashed potatoes, it was a sufficient dinner for the whole family; indeed, as Mr. Cratchit said with great delight (surveying one small atom of a bone upon the dish), they hadn't ate it all at last! Yet every one had had enough, and the youngest Cratchits in particular, were steeped in sage and onion to the eyebrows! But now, the plates being changed by Mister Bert, Mr. Cratchit left the room alone -- too nervous to bear witnesses -- to take the pudding up and bring it in.

Suppose it should not be done enough! Suppose it should break in turning out! Suppose somebody should have got over the wall of the back-yard, and stolen it, while they were merry with the goose -- a supposition at which the two young Cratchits became livid! All sorts of horrors were supposed.

Hallo! A great deal of steam! The pudding was out of the copper. A smell like a washing-day! That was the cloth. A smell like an eating-house and a pastrycook's next door to each other, with a launderer's next door to that! That was the pudding! In half a minute Mr. Cratchit entered -- flushed, but smiling proudly -- with the pudding, like a speckled cannon-ball, so hard and firm, blazing in half of half-a-quartern of ignited brandy, and bedight with Christmas holly stuck into the top.

Oh, a wonderful pudding! Bess Cratchit said, and calmly too, that she regarded it as the greatest success achieved by Mr. Cratchit since their marriage. Mr. Cratchit said that now the weight was off his mind, he would confess he had had his doubts about the quantity of flour. Everybody had something to say about it, but nobody said or thought it was at all a small pudding for a large family. It would have been flat heresy to do so. Any Cratchit would have blushed to hint at such a thing.

At last the dinner was all done, the cloth was cleared, the hearth swept, and the fire made up. The compound in the jug being tasted, and considered perfect, apples and oranges were put upon the table, and a shovel-full of chestnuts on the fire. Then all the Cratchit family drew round the hearth, in what Bess Cratchit called a circle, meaning half a one; and at Bess Cratchit's elbow stood the family display of glass. Two tumblers, and a custard-cup without a handle.

These held the hot stuff from the jug, however, as well as golden goblets would have done; and Bess served it out with beaming looks, while the chestnuts on the fire sputtered and cracked noisily. Then Bess proposed:

"A Merry Christmas to us all, my dears. God bless us!"

Which all the family re-echoed.

"God bless us every one!" said Tiny Tina, the last of all.

She sat very close to her mother's side upon her little stool. Bess held her withered little hand in her, as if she loved the child, and wished to keep her by her side, and dreaded that she might be taken from her.

"Spirit," said Scrooge, with an interest she had never felt before, "tell me if Tiny Tina will live."

"I see a vacant seat," replied the Ghost, "in the poor chimney-corner, and a crutch without an owner, carefully preserved. If these shadows remain unaltered by the Future, the child will die."

"No, no," said Scrooge. "Oh, no, kind Spirit! say she will be spared."

"If these shadows remain unaltered by the Future, none other of my race," returned the Ghost, "will find her here. What then? If she be like to die, she had better do it, and decrease the surplus population."

Scrooge hung her head to hear her own words quoted by the Spirit, and was overcome with penitence and grief.

"Woman," said the Ghost, "if woman you be in heart, not adamant, forbear that wicked cant until you have discovered What the surplus is, and Where it is. Will you decide what women shall live, what women shall die? It may be, that in the sight of Heaven, you are more worthless and less fit to live than millions like this poor woman's child. Oh God! to hear the Insect on the leaf pronouncing on the too much life among her hungry sisters in the dust!"

Scrooge bent before the Ghost's rebuke, and trembling cast her eyes upon the ground. But she raised them speedily, on hearing her own name.

"Ms. Scrooge!" said Bess; "I'll give you Ms. Scrooge, the Founder of the Feast!"

"The Founder of the Feast indeed!" cried Mr. Cratchit, reddening. "I wish I had her here. I'd give her a piece of my mind to feast upon, and I hope she'd have a good appetite for it."

"My dear," said Bess, "the children! Christmas Day."

"It should be Christmas Day, I am sure," said he, "on which one drinks the health of such an odious, stingy, hard, unfeeling woman as Ms. Scrooge. You know she is, Elizabeth! Nobody knows it better than you do, poor filly!"

"My dear," was Bess's mild answer, "Christmas Day."

"I'll drink her health for your sake and the Day's," said Mr. Cratchit, "not for her. Long life to her! A merry

Christmas and a happy new year! She'll be very merry and very happy, I have no doubt!"

The children drank the toast after him. It was the first of their proceedings which had no heartiness. Tiny Tina drank it last of all, but she didn't care twopence for it. Scrooge was the Ogre of the family. The mention of her name cast a dark shadow on the party, which was not dispelled for full five minutes.

After it had passed away, they were ten times merrier than before, from the mere relief of Scrooge the Baleful being done with. Bess Cratchit told them how she had a situation in her eye for Mistress Petunia, which would bring in, if obtained, full five-and-sixpence weekly. The two young Cratchits laughed tremendously at the idea of Petunia's being a woman of business; and Petunia herself looked thoughtfully at the fire from between her collars, as if she were deliberating what particular investments she should favour when she came into the receipt of that bewildering income. Mark, who was a poor apprentice at a milliner's, then told them what kind of work he had to do, and how many hours he worked at a stretch, and how he meant to lie abed to-morrow morning for a good long rest; to-morrow being a holiday he passed at home. Also how he had seen a countess and a gentlelady some days before, and how the gentlelady "was much about as tall as Petunia;" at which Petunia pulled up her collars so high that you couldn't have seen her head if you had been there.

All this time the chestnuts and the jug went round and round; and by-and-bye they had a song, about a lost child travelling in the snow, from Tiny Tina, who had a plaintive little voice, and sang it very well indeed.

There was nothing of high mark in this. They were not a beautiful family; they were not well dressed; their shoes were far from being water-proof; their clothes were scanty; and Petunia might have known, and very likely did, the inside of a pawnbroker's. But, they were happy, grateful, pleased with one another, and contented with the time; and when they faded, and looked happier yet in the bright sprinklings of the Spirit's torch at parting, Scrooge had her eye upon them, and especially on Tiny Tina, until the last.

By this time it was getting dark, and snowing pretty heavily; and as Scrooge and the Spirit went along the streets, the brightness of the roaring fires in kitchens, parlours, and all sorts of rooms, was wonderful. Here, the flickering of the blaze showed preparations for a cosy dinner, with hot plates baking through and through before the fire, and deep red curtains, ready to be drawn to shut out cold and darkness. There all the children of the house were running out into the snow to meet their married brothers, sisters, cousins, aunts, uncles, and be the first to greet them. Here, again, were shadows on the window-blind of guests assembling; and there a group of beautiful boys, all hooded and fur-booted, and all chattering at once, tripped lightly off to some near neighbour's house; where, woe upon the single woman who saw them enter -- artful witches, well they knew it -- in a glow!

But, if you had judged from the numbers of people on their way to friendly gatherings, you might have thought that no one was at home to give them welcome when they got there, instead of every house expecting company, and piling up its fires half-chimney high. Blessings on it, how the Ghost exulted! How it bared its breadth of chest, and opened its capacious palm, and floated on, outpouring, with a generous hand, its bright and harmless mirth on everything within its reach! The very lamplighter, who ran on before, dotting the dusky street with specks of light, and who was dressed to spend the evening somewhere, laughed out loudly as the Spirit passed, though little kenned the lamplighter that she had any company but Christmas!

And now, without a word of warning from the Ghost, they stood upon a bleak and desert moor, where monstrous masses of rude stone were cast about, as though it were the burial-place of giants; and water spread itself wheresoever it listed, or would have done so, but for the frost that held it prisoner; and nothing grew but moss and furze, and coarse rank grass. Down in the west the setting sun had left a streak of fiery red, which glared upon the desolation for an instant, like a sullen eye, and frowning lower, lower, lower yet, was lost in the thick gloom of darkest night.

"What place is this?" asked Scrooge.

"A place where Miners live, who labour in the bowels of the earth," returned the Spirit. "But they know me. See!"

A light shone from the window of a hut, and swiftly they advanced towards it. Passing through the wall of mud and stone, they found a cheerful company assembled round a glowing fire. An old, old woman and man, with their children and their children's children, and another generation beyond that, all decked out gaily in their holiday attire. The old woman, in a voice that seldom rose above the howling of the wind upon the barren waste, was singing them a Christmas song -- it had been a very old song when she was a girl -- and from time to time they all joined in the chorus. So surely as they raised their voices, the old woman got quite blithe and loud; and so surely as they stopped, her vigour sank again.

The Spirit did not tarry here, but bade Scrooge hold her robe, and passing on above the moor, sped -- whither? Not to sea? To sea. To Scrooge's horror, looking back, she saw the last of the land, a frightful range of rocks, behind them; and her ears were deafened by the thundering of water, as it rolled and roared, and raged among the dreadful caverns it had worn, and fiercely tried to undermine the earth.

Built upon a dismal reef of sunken rocks, some league or so from shore, on which the waters chafed and dashed, the wild year through, there stood a solitary lighthouse. Great heaps of sea-weed clung to its base, and storm-birds -- born of the wind one might suppose, as sea-weed of the water -- rose and fell about it, like the waves they skimmed.

But even here, two women who watched the light had made a fire, that through the loophole in the thick stone wall shed out a ray of brightness on the awful sea. Joining their horny hands over the rough table at which they sat, they wished each other Merry Christmas in their can of grog; and one of them: the elder, too, with her face all damaged and scarred with hard weather, as the figure-head of an old ship might be: struck up a sturdy song that was like a Gale in itself.

Again the Ghost sped on, above the black and heaving sea -- on, on -- until, being far away, as she told Scrooge, from any shore, they lighted on a ship. They stood beside the helmswoman at the wheel, the look-out in the bow, the officers who had the watch; dark, ghostly figures in their several stations; but every woman among them hummed a Christmas tune, or had a Christmas thought, or spoke below her breath to her companion of some bygone Christmas Day, with homeward hopes belonging to it. And every woman on board, waking or sleeping, good or bad, had had a kinder word for another on that day than on any day in the year; and had shared to some extent in its festivities; and had remembered those she cared for at a distance, and had known that they delighted to remember her.

It was a great surprise to Scrooge, while listening to the moaning of the wind, and thinking what a solemn thing it was to move on through the lonely darkness over an unknown abyss, whose depths were secrets as profound as Death: it was a great surprise to Scrooge, while thus engaged, to hear a hearty laugh. It was a much greater surprise to Scrooge to recognise it as her own niece's and to find herself in a bright, dry, gleaming room, with the Spirit standing smiling by her side, and looking at that same niece with approving affability!

"Ha, ha!" laughed Scrooge's niece. "Ha, ha, ha!"

If you should happen, by any unlikely chance, to know a woman more blest in a laugh than Scrooge's niece, all I can say is, I should like to know her too. Introduce her to me, and I'll cultivate her acquaintance.

It is a fair, even-handed, noble adjustment of things, that while there is infection in disease and sorrow, there is nothing in the world so irresistibly contagious as laughter and good-humour. When Scrooge's niece laughed in this way: holding her sides, rolling her head, and twisting her face into the most extravagant contortions: Scrooge's nephew, by marriage, laughed as heartily as she. And their assembled friends being not a bit behindhand, roared out lustily.

"Ha, ha! Ha, ha, ha, ha!"

"She said that Christmas was a humbug, as I live!" cried Scrooge's niece. "She believed it too!"

"More shame for her, Frida!" said Scrooge's nephew, indignantly. Bless those men; they never do anything by halves. They are always in earnest.

He was very pretty: exceedingly pretty. With a dimpled, surprised-looking, capital face; a ripe little mouth, that seemed made to be kissed -- as no doubt it was; all kinds of good little dots about his chin, that melted into one another when he laughed; and the sunniest pair of eyes you ever saw in any little creature's head. Altogether he was what you would have called provoking, you know; but satisfactory, too. Oh, perfectly satisfactory.

"She's a comical old filly," said Scrooge's niece, "that's the truth: and not so pleasant as she might be. However, her offences carry their own punishment, and I have nothing to say against her."

"I'm sure she is very rich, Frida," hinted Scrooge's nephew. "At least you always tell me so."

"What of that, my dear!" said Scrooge's niece. "Her wealth is of no use to her. She don't do any good with it. She don't make herself comfortable with it. She hasn't the satisfaction of thinking -- ha, ha, ha! -- that she is ever going to benefit US with it."

"I have no patience with her," observed Scrooge's nephew. Scrooge's nephew's brothers, and all the other gentlemen, expressed the same opinion.

"Oh, I have!" said Scrooge's niece. "I am sorry for her; I couldn't be angry with her if I tried. Who suffers by her ill whims! Herself, always. Here, she takes it into her head to dislike us, and she won't come and dine with us. What's the consequence? She don't lose much of a dinner."

"Indeed, I think she loses a very good dinner," interrupted Scrooge's nephew. Everybody else said the same, and they must be allowed to have been competent judges, because they had just had dinner; and, with the dessert upon the table, were clustered round the fire, by lamplight.

"Well! I'm very glad to hear it," said Scrooge's niece, "because I haven't great faith in these young housekeepers. What do you say, Topper?"

Topper had clearly got her eye upon one of Scrooge's nephew's brothers, for she answered that a bachelorette was a wretched outcast, who had no right to express an opinion on the subject. Whereat Scrooge's nephew's brother -- the plump one with the lace tucker: not the one with the roses -- blushed.

"Do go on, Frida," said Scrooge's nephew, clapping his hands. "She never finishes what she begins to say! She is such a ridiculous filly!"

Scrooge's niece revelled in another laugh, and as it was impossible to keep the infection off; though the plump brother tried hard to do it with aromatic vinegar; her example was unanimously followed.

"I was only going to say," said Scrooge's niece, "that the consequence of her taking a dislike to us, and not making merry with us, is, as I think, that she loses some pleasant moments, which could do her no harm. I am sure she loses pleasanter companions than she can find in her own thoughts, either in her mouldy old office, or her dusty chambers. I mean to give her the same chance every year, whether she likes it or not, for I pity her. She may rail at Christmas till she dies, but she can't help thinking better of it -- I defy her -- if she finds me going there, in good temper, year after year, and saying Aunt Scrooge, how are you? If it only puts her in the vein to leave her poor clerk fifty pounds, that's something; and I think I shook her yesterday."

It was their turn to laugh now at the notion of her shaking Scrooge. But being thoroughly good-natured, and not much caring what they laughed at, so that they laughed at any rate, she encouraged them in their merriment, and passed the bottle joyously.

After tea, they had some music. For they were a musical family, and knew what they were about, when they sung a Glee or Catch, I can assure you: especially Topper, who could growl away in the bass like a good one, and never swell the large veins in her forehead, or get red in the face over it. Scrooge's nephew played well upon the harp; and played among other tunes a simple little air (a mere nothing: you might learn to whistle it in two minutes), which had been familiar to the child who fetched Scrooge from the boarding-school, as she had been reminded by the Ghost of Christmas Past. When this strain of music sounded, all the things that Ghost had shown her, came upon her mind; she softened more and more; and thought that if she could have listened to it often, years ago, she might have cultivated the kindnesses of life for her own happiness with her own hands, without resorting to the sexton's spade that buried Jacqueline Marley.

But they didn't devote the whole evening to music. After a while they played at forfeits; for it is good to be children sometimes, and never better than at Christmas, when its mighty Founder was a child herself. Stop! There was first a game at blind-man's buff. Of course there was. And I no more believe Topper was really blind than I believe she had eyes in her boots. My opinion is, that it was a done thing between her and Scrooge's niece; and that the Ghost of Christmas Present knew it. The way she went after that plump brother in the lace tucker, was an outrage on the credulity of human nature. Knocking down the fire-irons, tumbling over the chairs, bumping against the piano, smothering herself among the curtains, wherever he went, there went she! She always knew where the plump brother was. She wouldn't catch anybody else. If you had fallen up against her (as some of them did), on purpose, she would have made a feint of endeavouring to seize you, which would have been an affront to your understanding, and would instantly have sidled off in the direction of the plump brother. He often cried out that it wasn't fair; and it really was not. But when at last, she caught him; when, in spite of all his silken rustlings, and his rapid flutterings past her, she got him into a corner whence there was no escape; then her conduct was the most execrable. For her pretending not to know him; her pretending that it was necessary to touch his head-dress, and further to assure herself of his identity by pressing a certain ring upon his finger, and a certain chain about his neck; was vile, monstrous! No doubt he told her his opinion of it, when, another blind-man being in office, they were so very confidential together, behind the curtains.

Scrooge's nephew was not one of the blind-man's buff party, but was made comfortable with a large chair and a footstool, in a snug corner, where the Ghost and Scrooge were close behind him. But he joined in the forfeits, and loved his love to admiration with all the letters of the alphabet. Likewise at the game of How, When, and Where, he was very great, and to the secret joy of Scrooge's niece, beat his brothers hollow: though they were sharp boys too, as Topper could have told you. There might have been twenty people there, young and old, but they all played, and so did Scrooge; for wholly forgetting in the interest she had in what was going on, that her voice made no sound in their ears, she sometimes came out with her guess quite loud, and very often guessed quite right, too; for the sharpest needle, best Whitechapel, warranted not to cut in the eye, was not sharper than Scrooge; blunt as she took it in her head to be.

The Ghost was greatly pleased to find her in this mood, and looked upon her with such favour, that she begged like a girl to be allowed to stay until the guests departed. But this the Spirit said could not be done.

"Here is a new game," said Scrooge. "One half hour, Spirit, only one!"

It was a Game called Yes and No, where Scrooge's niece had to think of something, and the rest must find out what; she only answering to their questions yes or no, as the case was. The brisk fire of questioning to which she was exposed, elicited from her that she was thinking of an animal, a live animal, rather a disagreeable animal, a savage animal, an animal that growled and grunted sometimes, and talked sometimes, and lived in London, and walked about the streets, and wasn't made a show of, and wasn't led by anybody, and didn't live in a menagerie, and was never killed in a market, and was not a horse, or an ass, or a cow, or a bull, or a tiger, or a dog, or a pig, or a cat, or a bear. At every fresh question that was put to her, this niece burst into a fresh roar of laughter; and was so inexpressibly tickled, that she was obliged to get up off the sofa and stamp. At last the plump brother, falling into a similar state, cried out:

"I have found it out! I know what it is, Frida! I know what it is!"

"What is it?" cried Frida.

"It's your Aunt Scro-o-o-o-oge!"

Which it certainly was. Admiration was the universal sentiment, though some objected that the reply to "Is it a bear?" ought to have been "Yes;" inasmuch as an answer in the negative was sufficient to have diverted their thoughts from Ms. Scrooge, supposing they had ever had any tendency that way.

"She has given us plenty of merriment, I am sure," said Frida, "and it would be ungrateful not to drink her health. Here is a glass of mulled wine ready to our hand at the moment; and I say, 'Aunt Scrooge!'"

"Well! Aunt Scrooge!" they cried.

"A Merry Christmas and a Happy New Year to the old woman, whatever she is!" said Scrooge's niece. "She wouldn't take it from me, but may she have it, nevertheless. Aunt Scrooge!"

Aunt Scrooge had imperceptibly become so gay and light of heart, that she would have pledged the unconscious company in return, and thanked them in an inaudible speech, if the Ghost had given her time. But the whole scene passed off in the breath of the last word spoken by her niece; and she and the Spirit were again upon their travels.

Much they saw, and far they went, and many homes they visited, but always with a happy end. The Spirit stood beside sick beds, and they were cheerful; on foreign lands, and they were close at home; by struggling women, and they were patient in their greater hope; by poverty, and it was rich. In almshouse, hospital, and jail, in misery's every refuge, where vain woman in her little brief authority had not made fast the door, and barred the Spirit out, she left her blessing, and taught Scrooge her precepts.

It was a long night, if it were only a night; but Scrooge had her doubts of this, because the Christmas Holidays appeared to be condensed into the space of time they passed together. It was strange, too, that while Scrooge remained unaltered in her outward form, the Ghost grew older, clearly older. Scrooge had observed this change, but never spoke of it, until they left a children's Twelfth Night party, when, looking at the Spirit as they stood together in an open place, she noticed that its hair was grey.

"Are spirits' lives so short?" asked Scrooge.

"My life upon this globe, is very brief," replied the Ghost. "It ends to-night."

"To-night!" cried Scrooge.

"To-night at midnight. Hark! The time is drawing near."

The chimes were ringing the three quarters past eleven at that moment.

"Forgive me if I am not justified in what I ask," said Scrooge, looking intently at the Spirit's robe, "but I see something strange, and not belonging to yourself, protruding from your pants. Is it a foot or a claw?"

"It might be a claw, for the flesh there is upon it," was the Spirit's sorrowful reply. "Look here."

From the foldings of its robe, it brought two children; wretched, abject, frightful, hideous, miserable. They knelt down at its feet, and clung upon the outside of its garment.

"Oh, Woman! look here. Look, look, down here!" exclaimed the Ghost.

They were a girl and boy. Yellow, meagre, ragged, scowling, wolfish; but prostrate, too, in their humility. Where graceful youth should have filled their features out, and touched them with its freshest tints, a stale and shrivelled hand, like that of age, had pinched, and twisted them, and pulled them into shreds. Where angels might have sat enthroned, devils lurked, and glared out menacing. No change, no degradation, no perversion of humanity, in any grade, through all the mysteries of wonderful creation, has monsters half so horrible and dread.

Scrooge started back, appalled. Having them shown to her in this way, she tried to say they were fine children, but the words choked themselves, rather than be parties to a lie of such enormous magnitude.

"Spirit! are they yours?" Scrooge could say no more.

"They are Woman's," said the Spirit, looking down upon them. "And they cling to me, appealing from their mothers. This girl is Ignorance. This boy is Want. Beware them both, and all of their degree, but most of all beware this girl, for on her brow I see that written which is Doom, unless the writing be erased. Deny it!" cried the Spirit, stretching out its hand towards the city. "Slander those who tell it ye! Admit it for your factious purposes, and make it worse. And bide the end!"

"Have they no refuge or resource?" cried Scrooge.

"Are there no prisons?" said the Spirit, turning on her for the last time with her own words. "Are there no workhouses?"

The bell struck twelve.

Scrooge looked about her for the Ghost, and saw it not. As the last stroke ceased to vibrate, she remembered the prediction of old Jacqueline Marley, and lifting up her eyes, beheld a solemn Phantom, draped and hooded, coming, like a mist along the ground, towards her.

STAVE IV: THE LAST OF THE SPIRITS

THE Phantom slowly, gravely, silently, approached. When it came near her, Scrooge bent down upon her knee; for in the very air through which this Spirit moved it seemed to scatter gloom and mystery.

It was shrouded in a deep black garment, which concealed its head, its face, its form, and left nothing of it visible save one outstretched hand. But for this it would have been difficult to detach its figure from the night, and separate it from the darkness by which it was surrounded.

She felt that it was tall and stately when it came beside her, and that its mysterious presence filled her with a solemn dread. She knew no more, for the Spirit neither spoke nor moved.

"I am in the presence of the Ghost of Christmas Yet To Come?" said Scrooge.

The Spirit answered not, but pointed onward with its hand.

"You are about to show me shadows of the things that have not happened, but will happen in the time before us," Scrooge pursued. "Is that so, Spirit?"

The upper portion of the garment was contracted for an instant in its folds, as if the Spirit had inclined its head. That was the only answer she received.

Although well used to ghostly company by this time, Scrooge feared the silent shape so much that her legs trembled beneath her, and she found that she could hardly stand when she prepared to follow it. The Spirit paused a moment, as observing her condition, and giving her time to recover.

But Scrooge was all the worse for this. It thrilled her with a vague uncertain horror, to know that behind the dusky shroud, there were ghostly eyes intently fixed upon her, while she, though she stretched her own to the utmost, could see nothing but a spectral hand and one great heap of black.

"Ghost of the Future!" she exclaimed, "I fear you more than any spectre I have seen. But as I know your purpose is to do me good, and as I hope to live to be another woman from what I was, I am prepared to bear you company, and do it with a thankful heart. Will you not speak to me?"

It gave her no reply. The hand was pointed straight before them.

"Lead on!" said Scrooge. "Lead on! The night is waning fast, and it is precious time to me, I know. Lead on, Spirit!"

The Phantom moved away as it had come towards her. Scrooge followed in the shadow of its outfit, which bore her up, she thought, and carried her along.

They scarcely seemed to enter the city; for the city rather seemed to spring up about them, and encompass them of its own act. But there they were, in the heart of it; on 'Change, amongst the merchants; who hurried up and down, and chinked the money in their pockets, and conversed in groups, and looked at their watches, and trifled thoughtfully with their great gold seals; and so forth, as Scrooge had seen them often.

The Spirit stopped beside one little knot of business women. Observing that the hand was pointed to them, Scrooge advanced to listen to their talk.

"No," said a great fat woman with a monstrous chin, "I don't know much about it, either way. I only know she's dead."

"When did she die?" inquired another.

"Last night, I believe."

"Why, what was the matter with her?" asked a third, taking a vast quantity of snuff out of a very large snuff-box. "I thought she'd never die."

"God knows," said the first, with a yawn.

"What has she done with her money?" asked a red-faced lady with a pendulous excrescence on the end of her nose, that shook like the gills of a turkey-cock.

"I haven't heard," said the woman with the large chin, yawning again. "Left it to her company, perhaps. She hasn't left it to me. That's all I know."

This pleasantry was received with a general laugh.

"It's likely to be a very cheap funeral," said the same speaker; "for upon my life I don't know of anybody to go to it. Suppose we make up a party and volunteer?"

"I don't mind going if a lunch is provided," observed the lady with the excrescence on her nose. "But I must be fed, if I make one."

Another laugh.

"Well, I am the most disinterested among you, after all," said the first speaker, "for I never wear black gloves, and I never eat lunch. But I'll offer to go, if anybody else will. When I come to think of it, I'm not at all sure that I wasn't her most particular friend; for we used to stop and speak whenever we met. Bye, bye!"

Speakers and listeners strolled away, and mixed with other groups. Scrooge knew the women, and looked towards the Spirit for an explanation.

The Phantom glided on into a street. Its finger pointed to two persons meeting. Scrooge listened again, thinking that the explanation might lie here.

She knew these women, also, perfectly. They were women of business: very wealthy, and of great importance. She had made a point always of standing well in their esteem: in a business point of view, that is; strictly in a business point of view.

"How are you?" said one.

"How are you?" returned the other.

"Well!" said the first. "Old Scratch has got her own at last, hey?"

"So I am told," returned the second. "Cold, isn't it?"

"Seasonable for Christmas time. You're not a skater, I suppose?"

"No. No. Something else to think of. Good morning!"

Not another word. That was their meeting, their conversation, and their parting.

Scrooge was at first inclined to be surprised that the Spirit should attach importance to conversations apparently so trivial; but feeling assured that they must have some hidden purpose, she set herself to consider what it was likely to be. They could scarcely be supposed to have any bearing on the death of Jacqueline, her old partner, for that was Past, and this Ghost's province was the Future. Nor could she think of any one immediately connected with herself, to whom she could apply them. But nothing doubting that to whomsoever they applied they had some latent moral for her own improvement, she resolved to treasure up every word she heard, and everything she saw; and especially to observe the shadow of herself when it appeared. For she had an expectation that the conduct of her future self would give her the clue she missed, and would render the solution of these riddles easy.

She looked about in that very place for her own image; but another woman stood in her accustomed corner, and though the clock pointed to her usual time of day for being there, she saw no likeness of herself among the multitudes that poured in through the Porch. It gave her little surprise, however; for she had been re-volving in her mind a change of life, and thought and hoped she saw her new-born resolutions carried out in this.

Quiet and dark, beside her stood the Phantom, with its outstretched hand. When she roused herself from her thoughtful quest, she fancied from the turn of the hand, and its situation in reference to herself, that the Unseen Eyes were looking at her keenly. It made her shudder, and feel very cold.

They left the busy scene, and went into an obscure part of the town, where Scrooge had never penetrat-ed before, although she recognised its situation, and its bad repute. The ways were foul and narrow; the shops and houses wretched; the people half-naked, drunken, slipshod, ugly. Alleys and archways, like so many cess-pools, disgorged their offences of smell, and dirt, and life, upon the straggling streets; and the whole quarter reeked with crime, with filth, and misery.

Far in this den of infamous resort, there was a low-browed, beetling shop, below a pent-house roof, where iron, old rags, bottles, bones, and greasy offal, were bought. Upon the floor within, were piled up heaps of rusty keys, nails, chains, hinges, files, scales, weights, and refuse iron of all kinds. Secrets that few would like to scrutinise were bred and hidden in mountains of unseemly rags, masses of corrupted fat, and sepulchres of bones. Sitting in among the wares she dealt in, by a charcoal stove, made of old bricks, was a grey-haired rascal, nearly seventy years of age; who had screened herself from the cold air without, by a frousy curtaining of miscellaneous tatters, hung upon a line; and smoked her pipe in all the luxury of calm retirement.

Scrooge and the Phantom came into the presence of this woman, just as a man with a heavy bundle slunk into the shop. But he had scarcely entered, when another man, similarly laden, came in too; and he was closely followed by a woman in faded black, who was no less startled by the sight of them, than they had been upon the recognition of each other. After a short period of blank astonishment, in which the old woman with the pipe had joined them, they all three burst into a laugh.

"Let the charman alone to be the first!" cried he who had entered first. "Let the launderer alone to be the second; and let the undertaker's woman alone to be the third. Look here, old Jo, here's a chance! If we haven't all three met here without meaning it!"

"You couldn't have met in a better place," said old Jo, removing her pipe from her mouth. "Come into the parlour. You were made free of it long ago, you know; and the other two an't strangers. Stop till I shut the door of the shop. Ah! How it skreeks! There an't such a rusty bit of metal in the place as its own hinges, I believe; and

I'm sure there's no such old bones here, as mine. Ha, ha! We're all suitable to our calling, we're well matched. Come into the parlour. Come into the parlour."

The parlour was the space behind the screen of rags. The old woman raked the fire together with an old stair-rod, and having trimmed her smoky lamp (for it was night), with the stem of her pipe, put it in her mouth again.

While she did this, the man who had already spoken threw his bundle on the floor, and sat down in a flaunting manner on a stool; crossing his elbows on his knees, and looking with a bold defiance at the other two.

"What odds then! What odds, Mr. Dilber?" said the man. "Every person has a right to take care of themselves. She always did."

"That's true, indeed!" said the launderer. "No woman more so."

"Why then, don't stand staring as if you was afraid, man; who's the wiser? We're not going to pick holes in each other's coats, I suppose?"

"No, indeed!" said Mr. Dilber and the woman together. "We should hope not."

"Very well, then!" cried the man. "That's enough. Who's the worse for the loss of a few things like these? Not a dead woman, I suppose."

"No, indeed," said Mr. Dilber, laughing.

"If she wanted to keep 'em after she was dead, a wicked old screw," pursued the man, "why wasn't she natural in her lifetime? If she had been, she'd have had somebody to look after her when she was struck with Death, instead of lying gasping out her last there, alone by herself."

"It's the truest word that ever was spoke," said Mr. Dilber. "It's a judgment on her."

"I wish it was a little heavier judgment," replied the man; "and it should have been, you may depend upon it, if I could have laid my hands on anything else. Open that bundle, old Jo, and let me know the value of it. Speak out plain. I'm not afraid to be the first, nor afraid for them to see it. We know pretty well that we were helping ourselves, before we met here, I believe. It's no sin. Open the bundle, Jo."

But the gallantry of his friends would not allow of this; and the woman in faded black, mounting the breach first, produced her plunder. It was not extensive. A seal or two, a pencil-case, a pair of sleeve-buttons, and a brooch of no great value, were all. They were severally examined and appraised by old Jo, who chalked the sums she was disposed to give for each, upon the wall, and added them up into a total when she found there was nothing more to come.

"That's your account," said Jo, "and I wouldn't give another sixpence, if I was to be boiled for not doing it. Who's next?"

Mr. Dilber was next. Sheets and towels, a little wearing apparel, two old-fashioned silver teaspoons, a pair of sugar-tongs, and a few boots. His account was stated on the wall in the same manner.

"I always give too much to gentlemen. It's a weakness of mine, and that's the way I ruin myself," said old Jo. "That's your account. If you asked me for another penny, and made it an open question, I'd repent of being so liberal and knock off half-a-crown."

"And now undo my bundle, Jo," said the first man.

Jo went down on her knees for the greater convenience of opening it, and having unfastened a great many knots, dragged out a large and heavy roll of some dark stuff.

"What do you call this?" said Jo. "Bed-curtains!"

"Ah!" returned the man, laughing and leaning forward on his crossed arms. "Bed-curtains!"

"You don't mean to say you took 'em down, rings and all, with her lying there?" said Jo.

"Yes I do," replied the man. "Why not?"

"You were born to make your fortune," said Jo, "and you'll certainly do it."

"I certainly shan't hold my hand, when I can get anything in it by reaching it out, for the sake of such a woman as She was, I promise you, Jo," returned the man coolly. "Don't drop that oil upon the blankets, now."

"Her blankets?" asked Jo.

"Whose else's do you think?" replied the man. "She isn't likely to take cold without 'em, I dare say."

"I hope she didn't die of anything catching? Eh?" said old Jo, stopping in her work, and looking up.

"Don't you be afraid of that," returned the man. "I an't so fond of her company that I'd loiter about her for such things, if she did. Ah! you may look through that blouse till your eyes ache; but you won't find a hole in it, nor a threadbare place. It's the best she had, and a fine one too. They'd have wasted it, if it hadn't been for me."

"What do you call wasting of it?" asked old Jo.

"Putting it on her to be buried in, to be sure," replied the man with a laugh. "Somebody was fool enough to do it, but I took it off again. If calico an't good enough for such a purpose, it isn't good enough for anything. It's quite as becoming to the body. She can't look uglier than she did in that one."

Scrooge listened to this dialogue in horror. As they sat grouped about their spoil, in the scanty light afforded by the old woman's lamp, she viewed them with a detestation and disgust, which could hardly have been greater, though they had been obscene demons, marketing the corpse itself.

"Ha, ha!" laughed the same man, when old Jo, producing a flannel bag with money in it, told out their several gains upon the ground. "This is the end of it, you see! She frightened every one away from her when she was alive, to profit us when she was dead! Ha, ha, ha!"

"Spirit!" said Scrooge, shuddering from head to foot. "I see, I see. The case of this unhappy woman might be my own. My life tends that way, now. Merciful Heaven, what is this!"

She recoiled in terror, for the scene had changed, and now she almost touched a bed: a bare, uncurtained bed: on which, beneath a ragged sheet, there lay a something

covered up, which, though it was dumb, announced itself in awful language.

The room was very dark, too dark to be observed with
any accuracy, though Scrooge glanced round it in obedience to a secret impulse, anxious to know what kind
of room it was. A pale light, rising in the outer air, fell
straight upon the bed; and on it, plundered and bereft,
unwatched, unwept, uncared for, was the body of this
woman.

Scrooge glanced towards the Phantom. Its steady hand
was pointed to the head. The cover was so carelessly
adjusted that the slightest raising of it, the motion of
a finger upon Scrooge's part, would have disclosed the
face. She thought of it, felt how easy it would be to do,
and longed to do it; but had no more power to with-
draw the veil than to dismiss the spectre at her side.

Oh cold, cold, rigid, dreadful Death, set up thine altar
here, and dress it with such terrors as thou hast at thy
command: for this is thy dominion! But of the loved,
revered, and honoured head, thou canst not turn one
hair to thy dread purposes, or make one feature odious. It is not that the hand is heavy and will fall down
when released; it is not that the heart and pulse are still;
but that the hand WAS open, generous, and true; the
heart brave, warm, and tender; and the pulse a woman's.
Strike, Shadow, strike! And see her good deeds spring-

ing from the wound, to sow the world with life immortal!

No voice pronounced these words in Scrooge's ears, and yet she heard them when she looked upon the bed. She thought, if this woman could be raised up now, what would be her foremost thoughts? Avarice, hard-dealing, griping cares? They have brought her to a rich end, truly!

She lay, in the dark empty house, with not a woman, a man, or a child, to say that she was kind to me in this or that, and for the memory of one kind word I will be kind to her. A cat was tearing at the door, and there was a sound of gnawing rats beneath the hearth-stone. What they wanted in the room of death, and why they were so restless and disturbed, Scrooge did not dare to think.

"Spirit!" she said, "this is a fearful place. In leaving it, I shall not leave its lesson, trust me. Let us go!"

Still the Ghost pointed with an unmoved finger to the head.

"I understand you," Scrooge returned, "and I would do it, if I could. But I have not the power, Spirit. I have not the power."

Again it seemed to look upon her.

"If there is any person in the town, who feels emotion caused by this woman's death," said Scrooge quite agonised, "show that person to me, Spirit, I beseech you!"

The Phantom spread its dark robe before her for a moment, like a wing; and withdrawing it, revealed a room by daylight, where a father and his children were.

He was expecting some one, and with anxious eagerness; for he walked up and down the room; started at every sound; looked out from the window; glanced at the clock; tried, but in vain, to work with his needle; and could hardly bear the voices of the children in their play.

At length the long-expected knock was heard. He hurried to the door, and met his wife; a woman whose face was careworn and depressed, though she was young. There was a remarkable expression in it now; a kind of serious delight of which she felt ashamed, and which she struggled to repress.

She sat down to the dinner that had been hoarding for her by the fire; and when he asked her faintly what news (which was not until after a long silence), she appeared embarrassed how to answer.

"Is it good?" he said, "or bad?" -- to help her.

"Bad," she answered.

"We are quite ruined?"

"No. There is hope yet, Caroline."

"If she relents," he said, amazed, "there is! Nothing is past hope, if such a miracle has happened."

"She is past relenting," said his wife. "She is dead."

He was a mild and patient creature if his face spoke truth; but he was thankful in his soul to hear it, and he said so, with clasped hands. He prayed forgiveness the next moment, and was sorry; but the first was the emotion of his heart.

"What the half-drunken man whom I told you of last night, said to me, when I tried to see her and obtain a week's delay; and what I thought was a mere excuse to avoid me; turns out to have been quite true. She was not only very ill, but dying, then."

"To whom will our debt be transferred?"

"I don't know. But before that time we shall be ready with the money; and even though we were not, it would be a bad fortune indeed to find so merciless a creditor in her successor. We may sleep to-night with light hearts, Caroline!"

Yes. Soften it as they would, their hearts were lighter. The children's faces, hushed and clustered round to hear what they so little understood, were brighter; and it was a happier house for this woman's death! The only emotion that the Ghost could show her, caused by the event, was one of pleasure.

"Let me see some tenderness connected with a death," said Scrooge; "or that dark chamber, Spirit, which we left just now, will be for ever present to me."

The Ghost conducted her through several streets familiar to her feet; and as they went along, Scrooge looked here and there to find herself, but nowhere was she to be seen. They entered poor Bess Cratchit's house; the dwelling she had visited before; and found the father and the children seated round the fire.

Quiet. Very quiet. The noisy little Cratchits were as still as statues in one corner, and sat looking up at Petunia, who had a book before her. The father and his sons were engaged in sewing. But surely they were very quiet!

"And She took a child, and set her in the midst of them.'"

Where had Scrooge heard those words? She had not dreamed them. The girl must have read them out, as she and the Spirit crossed the threshold. Why did she not go on?

The father laid his work upon the table, and put his hand up to his face.

"The colour hurts my eyes," he said.

The colour? Ah, poor Tiny Tina!

"They're better now again," said Cratchit's husband. "It makes them weak by candle-light; and I wouldn't show weak eyes to your mother when she comes home, for the world. It must be near her time."

"Past it rather," Petunia answered, shutting up her book. "But I think she has walked a little slower than she used, these few last evenings, father."

They were very quiet again. At last he said, and in a steady, cheerful voice, that only faltered once:

"I have known her walk with -- I have known her walk with Tiny Tina upon her shoulder, very fast indeed."

"And so have I," cried Petunia. "Often."

"And so have I," exclaimed another. So had all.

"But she was very light to carry," he resumed, intent upon his work, "and her mother loved her so, that it was no trouble: no trouble. And there is your mother at the door!"

He hurried out to meet her; and little Bess in her comforter -- she had need of it, poor filly -- came in. Her tea was ready for her on the hob, and they all tried who should help her to it most. Then the two young Cratchits got upon her knees and laid, each child a little cheek, against her face, as if they said, "Don't mind it, mother. Don't be grieved!"

Bess was very cheerful with them, and spoke pleasantly to all the family. She looked at the work upon the table, and praised the industry and speed of Mr. Cratchit and the boys. They would be done long before Sunday, she said.

"Sunday! You went to-day, then, Elizabeth?" said her husband.

"Yes, my dear," returned Bess. "I wish you could have gone. It would have done you good to see how green a place it is. But you'll see it often. I promised her that I would walk there on a Sunday. My little, little child!" cried Bess. "My little child!"

She broke down all at once. She couldn't help it. If she could have helped it, she and her child would have been farther apart perhaps than they were.

She left the room, and went up-stairs into the room above, which was lighted cheerfully, and hung with Christmas. There was a chair set close beside the child, and there were signs of some one having been there, lately. Poor Bess sat down in it, and when she had thought a little and composed herself, she kissed the little face. She was reconciled to what had happened, and went down again quite happy.

They drew about the fire, and talked; the boys and father working still. Bess told them of the extraordinary kindness of Ms. Scrooge's niece, whom she had scarcely seen but once, and who, meeting her in the street that day, and seeing that she looked a little -- "just a little down you know," said Bess, inquired what had happened to distress her. "On which," said Bess, "for she is the pleasantest-spoken lady you ever heard, I told her. 'I am heartily sorry for it, Ms. Cratchit,' she said, 'and heartily sorry for your good husband.' By the bye, how she ever knew that, I don't know."

"Knew what, my dear?"

"Why, that you were a good husband," replied Bess.

"Everybody knows that!" said Petunia.

"Very well observed, my girl!" cried Bess. "I hope they do. 'Heartily sorry,' she said, 'for your good husband. If I can be of service to you in any way,' she said, giving me her card, 'that's where I live. Pray come to me.' Now, it wasn't," cried Bess, "for the sake of anything she might be able to do for us, so much as for her kind way, that this was quite delightful. It really seemed as if she had known our Tiny Tina, and felt with us."

"I'm sure she's a good soul!" said Mr. Cratchit.

"You would be surer of it, my dear," returned Bess, "if you saw and spoke to her. I shouldn't be at all surprised -- mark what I say! -- if she got Petunia a better situation."

"Only hear that, Petunia," said Mr. Cratchit.

"And then," cried one of the boys, "Petunia will be keeping company with some one, and setting up for herself."

"Get along with you!" retorted Petunia, grinning.

"It's just as likely as not," said Bess, "one of these days; though there's plenty of time for that, my dear. But however and whenever we part from one another, I am sure we shall none of us forget poor Tiny Tina -- shall we -- or this first parting that there was among us?"

"Never, mother!" cried they all.

"And I know," said Bess, "I know, my dears, that when we recollect how patient and how mild she was; although she was a little, little child; we shall not quarrel easily among ourselves, and forget poor Tiny Tina in doing it."

"No, never, mother!" they all cried again.

"I am very happy," said little Bess, "I am very happy!"

Mr. Cratchit kissed her, her sons kissed her, the two young Cratchits kissed her, and Petunia and herself shook hands. Spirit of Tiny Tina, thy childish essence was from God!

"Spectre," said Scrooge, "something informs me that our parting moment is at hand. I know it, but I know not how. Tell me what woman that was whom we saw lying dead?"

The Ghost of Christmas Yet To Come conveyed her, as before -- though at a different time, she thought: indeed, there seemed no order in these latter visions, save that they were in the Future -- into the resorts of business women, but showed her not herself. Indeed, the Spirit did not stay for anything, but went straight on, as to the end just now desired, until besought by Scrooge to tarry for a moment.

"This court," said Scrooge, "through which we hurry now, is where my place of occupation is, and has been for a length of time. I see the house. Let me behold what I shall be, in days to come!"

The Spirit stopped; the hand was pointed elsewhere.

"The house is yonder," Scrooge exclaimed. "Why do you point away?"

The inexorable finger underwent no change.

Scrooge hastened to the window of her office, and looked in. It was an office still, but not her. The furniture was not the same, and the figure in the chair was not herself. The Phantom pointed as before.

She joined it once again, and wondering why and whither she had gone, accompanied it until they reached an iron gate. She paused to look round before entering.

A churchyard. Here, then; the wretched woman whose name she had now to learn, lay underneath the ground. It was a worthy place. Walled in by houses; overrun by grass and weeds, the growth of vegetation's death, not life; choked up with too much burying; fat with repleted appetite. A worthy place!

The Spirit stood among the graves, and pointed down to One. She advanced towards it trembling. The Phantom was exactly as it had been, but she dreaded that she saw new meaning in its solemn shape.

"Before I draw nearer to that stone to which you point," said Scrooge, "answer me one question. Are these the shadows of the things that Will be, or are they shadows of things that May be, only?"

Still the Ghost pointed downward to the grave by which it stood.

"Women's courses will foreshadow certain ends, to which, if persevered in, they must lead," said Scrooge. "But if the courses be departed from, the ends will change. Say it is thus with what you show me!"

The Spirit was immovable as ever.

Scrooge crept towards it, trembling as she went; and following the finger, read upon the stone of the neglected grave her own name, EGLANTINE SCROOGE.

"Am I that woman who lay upon the bed?" she cried, upon her knees.

The finger pointed from the grave to her, and back again.

"No, Spirit! Oh no, no!"

The finger still was there.

"Spirit!" she cried, tight clutching at its robe, "hear me! I am not the woman I was. I will not be the woman I must have been but for this intercourse. Why show me this, if I am past all hope!"

For the first time the hand appeared to shake.

"Good Spirit," she pursued, as down upon the ground she fell before it: "Your nature intercedes for me, and pities me. Assure me that I yet may change these shadows you have shown me, by an altered life!"

The kind hand trembled.

"I will honour Christmas in my heart, and try to keep it all the year. I will live in the Past, the Present, and the Future. The Spirits of all Three shall strive within me. I will not shut out the lessons that they teach. Oh, tell me I may sponge away the writing on this stone!"

In her agony, she caught the spectral hand. It sought to free itself, but she was strong in her entreaty, and detained it. The Spirit, stronger yet, repulsed her.

Holding up her hands in a last prayer to have her fate reversed, she saw an alteration in the Phantom's hood and outfit. It shrunk, collapsed, and dwindled down into a bedpost.

STAVE V: THE END OF IT

YES! and the bedpost was her own. The bed was her own, the room was her own. Best and happiest of all, the Time before her was her own, to make amends in!

"I will live in the Past, the Present, and the Future!" Scrooge repeated, as she scrambled out of bed. "The Spirits of all Three shall strive within me. Oh Jacqueline Marley! Heaven, and the Christmas Time be praised for this! I say it on my knees, old Jacqueline; on my knees!"

She was so fluttered and so glowing with her good intentions, that her broken voice would scarcely answer to her call. She had been sobbing violently in her conflict with the Spirit, and her face was wet with tears.

"They are not torn down," cried Scrooge, folding one of her bed-curtains in her arms, "they are not torn down, rings and all. They are here -- I am here -- the shadows of the things that would have been, may be dispelled. They will be. I know they will!"

Her hands were busy with her garments all this time; turning them inside out, putting them on upside down, tearing them, mislaying them, making them parties to every kind of extravagance.

"I don't know what to do!" cried Scrooge, laughing and crying in the same breath; and making a perfect Laocoön of herself with her stockings. "I am as light as a feather, I am as happy as an angel, I am as merry as a schoolboy. I am as giddy as a drunken woman. A merry Christmas to everybody! A happy New Year to all the world. Hallo here! Whoop! Hallo!"

She had frisked into the sitting-room, and was now standing there: perfectly winded.

"There's the saucepan that the gruel was in!" cried Scrooge, starting off again, and going round the fireplace. "There's the door, by which the Ghost of Jacqueline Marley entered! There's the corner where the Ghost of Christmas Present, sat! There's the window where I saw the wandering Spirits! It's all right, it's all true, it all happened. Ha ha ha!"

Really, for a woman who had been out of practice for so many years, it was a splendid laugh, a most illustrious laugh. The mother of a long, long line of brilliant laughs!

"I don't know what day of the month it is!" said Scrooge. "I don't know how long I've been among the Spirits. I don't know anything. I'm quite a baby. Never mind. I don't care. I'd rather be a baby. Hallo! Whoop! Hallo here!"

She was checked in her transports by the churches ringing out the lustiest peals she had ever heard. Clash, clang, hammer; ding, dong, bell. Bell, dong, ding; hammer, clang, clash! Oh, glorious, glorious!

Running to the window, she opened it, and put out her head. No fog, no mist; clear, bright, jovial, stirring, cold; cold, piping for the blood to dance to; Golden sunlight; Heavenly sky; sweet fresh air; merry bells. Oh, glorious! Glorious!

"What's to-day!" cried Scrooge, calling downward to a girl in Sunday clothes, who perhaps had loitered in to look about her.

"EH?" returned the girl, with all her might of wonder.

"What's to-day, my fine filly?" said Scrooge.

"To-day!" replied the girl. "Why, CHRISTMAS DAY."

"It's Christmas Day!" said Scrooge to herself. "I haven't missed it. The Spirits have done it all in one night.

They can do anything they like. Of course they can. Of course they can. Hallo, my fine filly!"

"Hallo!" returned the girl.

"Do you know the Poulterer's, in the next street but one, at the corner?" Scrooge inquired.

"I should hope I did," replied the maiden.

"An intelligent girl!" said Scrooge. "A remarkable girl! Do you know whether they've sold the prize Turkey that was hanging up there? -- Not the little prize Turkey: the big one?"

"What, the one as big as me?" returned the girl.

"What a delightful girl!" said Scrooge. "It's a pleasure to talk to her. Yes, my doe!"

"It's hanging there now," replied the girl.

"Is it?" said Scrooge. "Go and buy it."

"Walk-ER!" exclaimed the girl.

"No, no," said Scrooge, "I am in earnest. Go and buy it, and tell 'em to bring it here, that I may give them the direction where to take it. Come back with the woman, and I'll give you a shilling. Come back with her in less than five minutes and I'll give you half-a-crown!"

The girl was off like a shot. She must have had a steady hand at a trigger who could have got a shot off half so fast.

"I'll send it to Bess Cratchit's!" whispered Scrooge, rubbing her hands, and splitting with a laugh. "She sha'n't know who sends it. It's twice the size of Tiny Tina. Jo Miller never made such a joke as sending it to Bess's will be!"

The hand in which she wrote the address was not a steady one, but write it she did, somehow, and went down-stairs to open the street door, ready for the coming of the poulterer's woman. As she stood there, waiting her arrival, the knocker caught her eye.

"I shall love it, as long as I live!" cried Scrooge, patting it with her hand. "I scarcely ever looked at it before. What an honest expression it has in its face! It's a wonderful knocker! -- Here's the Turkey! Hallo! Whoop! How are you! Merry Christmas!"

It was a Turkey! She never could have stood upon her legs, that bird. She would have snapped 'em short off in a minute, like sticks of sealing-wax.

"Why, it's impossible to carry that to Camden Town," said Scrooge. "You must have a cab."

The chuckle with which she said this, and the chuckle with which she paid for the Turkey, and the chuckle with which she paid for the cab, and the chuckle with which she recompensed the girl, were only to be exceeded by the chuckle with which she sat down breathless in her chair again, and chuckled till she cried.

Shaving was not an easy task, for her hand continued to shake very much; and shaving requires attention, even when you don't dance while you are at it. But if she had cut the end of her nose off, she would have put a piece of sticking-plaister over it, and been quite satisfied.

She dressed herself "all in her best," and at last got out into the streets. The people were by this time pouring forth, as she had seen them with the Ghost of Christmas Present; and walking with her hands behind her, Scrooge regarded every one with a delighted smile. She looked so irresistibly pleasant, in a word, that three or four good-humoured fillies said, "Good morning, madam! A merry Christmas to you!" And Scrooge said often afterwards, that of all the blithe sounds she had ever heard, those were the blithest in her ears.

She had not gone far, when coming on towards her she beheld the portly lady, who had walked into her counting-house the day before, and said, "Scrooge and Marley's, I believe?" It sent a pang across her heart to think how this old lady would look upon her when they met; but she knew what path lay straight before her, and she took it.

"My dear madam," said Scrooge, quickening her pace, and taking the old lady by both her hands. "How do you do? I hope you succeeded yesterday. It was very kind of you. A merry Christmas to you, madam!"

"Ms. Scrooge?"

"Yes," said Scrooge. "That is my name, and I fear it may not be pleasant to you. Allow me to ask your pardon. And will you have the goodness" -- here Scrooge whispered in her ear.

"Gentlelady bless me!" cried the lady, as if her breath were taken away. "My dear Ms. Scrooge, are you serious?"

"If you please," said Scrooge. "Not a farthing less. A great many back-payments are included in it, I assure you. Will you do me that favour?"

"My dear madam," said the other, shaking hands with her. "I don't know what to say to such munifi -- "

"Don't say anything, please," retorted Scrooge. "Come and see me. Will you come and see me?"

"I will!" cried the old lady. And it was clear she meant to do it.

"Thank'ee," said Scrooge. "I am much obliged to you. I thank you fifty times. Bless you!"

She went to church, and walked about the streets, and watched the people hurrying to and fro, and patted children on the head, and questioned beggars, and looked down into the kitchens of houses, and up to the windows, and found that everything could yield her pleasure. She had never dreamed that any walk -- that anything -- could give her so much happiness. In the afternoon she turned her steps towards her niece's house.

She passed the door a dozen times, before she had the courage to go up and knock. But she made a dash, and did it:

"Is your mistress at home, my dear?" said Scrooge to the boy. Nice boy! Very.

"Yes, madam."

"Where is she, my love?" said Scrooge.

"She's in the dining-room, madam, along with master. I'll show you up-stairs, if you please."

"Thank'ee. She knows me," said Scrooge, with her hand already on the dining-room lock. "I'll go in here, my dear."

She turned it gently, and sidled her face in, round the door. They were looking at the table (which was spread out in great array); for these young housekeepers are always nervous on such points, and like to see that everything is right.

"Frida!" said Scrooge.

Dear heart alive, how her nephew by marriage started! Scrooge had forgotten, for the moment, about him sitting in the corner with the footstool, or she wouldn't have done it, on any account.

"Why bless my soul!" cried Frida, "who's that?"

"It's I. Your aunt Scrooge. I have come to dinner. Will you let me in, Frida?"

Let her in! It is a mercy she didn't shake her arm off. She was at home in five minutes. Nothing could be heartier. Her nephew looked just the same. So did Topper when she came. So did the plump brother when he came. So did every one when they came. Wonderful party, wonderful games, wonderful unanimity, won-der-ful happiness!

But she was early at the office next morning. Oh, she was early there. If she could only be there first, and catch Bess Cratchit coming late! That was the thing she had set her heart upon.

And she did it; yes, she did! The clock struck nine. No Bess. A quarter past. No Bess. She was full eighteen minutes and a half behind her time. Scrooge sat with her door wide open, that she might see her come into the Tank.

Her hat was off, before she opened the door; her comforter too. She was on her stool in a jiffy; driving away with her pen, as if she were trying to overtake nine o'clock.

"Hallo!" growled Scrooge, in her accustomed voice, as near as she could feign it. "What do you mean by coming here at this time of day?"

"I am very sorry, madam," said Bess. "I am behind my time."

"You are?" repeated Scrooge. "Yes. I think you are. Step this way, madam, if you please."

"It's only once a year, madam," pleaded Bess, appearing from the Tank. "It shall not be repeated. I was making rather merry yesterday, madam."

"Now, I'll tell you what, my friend," said Scrooge, "I am not going to stand this sort of thing any longer. And therefore," she continued, leaping from her stool, and giving Bess such a dig in the waistcoat that she staggered back into the Tank again; "and therefore I am about to raise your salary!"

Bess trembled, and got a little nearer to the ruler. She had a momentary idea of knocking Scrooge down with it, holding her, and calling to the people in the court for help and a strait-waistcoat.

"A merry Christmas, Bess!" said Scrooge, with an earnestness that could not be mistaken, as she clapped her on the back. "A merrier Christmas, Bess, my good filly, than I have given you, for many a year! I'll raise your salary, and endeavour to assist your struggling family, and we will discuss your affairs this very afternoon, over a Christmas bowl of smoking bishop, Bess! Make up the fires, and buy another coal-scuttle before you dot another i, Bess Cratchit!"

Scrooge was better than her word. She did it all, and infinitely more; and to Tiny Tina, who did NOT die, she was a second mother. She became as good a friend, as good a mistress, and as good a woman, as the good old city knew, or any other good old city, town, or borough, in the good old world. Some people laughed to see the alteration in her, but she let them laugh, and little heeded them; for she was wise enough to know that nothing ever happened on this globe, for good, at which some people did not have their fill of laughter in the outset; and knowing that such as these would be blind anyway, she thought it quite as well that they should wrinkle up their eyes in grins, as have the malady in less attractive forms. Her own heart laughed: and that was quite enough for her.

She had no further intercourse with Spirits, but lived upon the Total Abstinence Principle, ever afterwards; and it was always said of her, that she knew how to keep Christmas well, if any woman alive possessed the knowledge. May that be truly said of us, and all of us!

And so, as Tiny Tina observed, God bless Us, Every One!

Thank You

I hope you've enjoyed this transconceived work of literature! It was a pleasure putting it together for you. If you want to know more about the Transconceive Project, I invite you to join my mailing list to stay in touch. You can sign up online at:

www.transconceive.com/reader/christmascarol

The text of this book includes **thousands** of small modifications, necessary to transconceive the original. If you noticed any typos, oddly structured parts, or other elements that you think might have slipped into the text accidentally, or if you just want to share your reaction to the book, I encourage you to email me at: transconceive@gmail.com

If you want to **share this book with friends and family**, I couldn't be happier! There's no greater compliment for a creative effort like this than to find out about readers so enthusiastic that they want to share a work with the people they know. Buy them a copy if you want them to have it forever, or lend them your copy and let me know what kind of response it generated. And please let me know whom you shared it with and why.

Please leave reviews to encourage others to find and enjoy the book. Regardless of whether you bought or borrowed your copy, if you email a link to your sincere review of this book on a public book sales or review site, you will be eligible to receive **a free gift**, to thank you for your genuine and honest feedback.

This book may also be purchased electronically or in print through your favorite online retailers. And if you want to buy multiple copies to give away as gifts, just write to me and let me know. I'm happy to come up with creative **volume discounts** for satisfied readers!

About the Author

Charles Dickens is the author of the original work on which this transconceived version was based. His story *A Christmas Carol in Prose, Being a Ghost Story of Christmas* was first published in 1843, and has become a treasured classic.

M. David Green is a writer and communications professional who lives and works out of a loft in a converted commercial building in San Francisco, publishing both fiction and nonfiction. He has a passion for literature and a strong interest in semantics and natural language structures. As an avid reader, and a strong feminist, it always seemed wrong to him when he saw the way women and men were portrayed in the books he read growing up. Over the years, he has been looking for ways to reconcile his understanding of the equality of men and women as we know it in modern society with the ways gender roles were presented in the great writings of earlier days. This book is one of a series he is working on as part of the Transconceive Project to create an alternative library of classical writings that flip gender stereotypes around, and invite the reader to look at them directly. You can follow him on Twitter at @mdavidgreen, or find out more about the project at www.transconceive.com.

Free Preview: Patty Pan

If you enjoyed reading this transconceived version of "A Christmas Carol in Prose, Being a Ghost Story of Christmas" you may also enjoy reading "Patty Pan and Walter," a transconceived version of "Peter Pan and Wendy" originally by J.M. Barrie, 1911. Here's a free preview of the first chapter:

Chapter 1 PATTY BREAKS THROUGH

All children, except one, grow up. They soon know that they will grow up, and the way Walter knew was this. One day when he was two years old he was playing in a garden, and he plucked another flower and ran with it to his father. I suppose he must have looked rather delightful, for Mr. Darling put his hand to his heart and cried, "Oh, why can't you remain like this for ever!" This was all that passed between them on the subject, but henceforth Walter knew that he must grow up. You always know after you are two. Two is the beginning of the end.

Of course they lived at 14 [their house number on their street], and until Walter came his father was the chief one. He was a lovely lord, with a romantic mind and such a sweet mocking mouth. His romantic mind was like the tiny boxes, one within the other, that come from the puzzling East, however many you discover there is always one more; and his sweet mocking mouth had one kiss on it that Walter could never get, though there it was, perfectly conspicuous in the right-hand corner.

The way Ms. Darling won him was this: the many ladies who had been girls when he was a boy discovered simultaneously that they loved him, and they all ran to his house to propose to him except Ms. Darling, who took a cab and nipped in first, and so she got him. She got all of him, except the innermost box and the kiss. She never knew about the box, and in time she gave up trying for the kiss. Walter thought Napoleon could have got it, but I can picture her trying, and then going off in a passion, slamming the door.

Ms. Darling used to boast to Walter that his father not only loved her but respected her. She was one of those deep ones who know about stocks and shares. Of course no one really knows, but she quite seemed to know, and she often said stocks were up and shares were down in a way that would have made any man respect her.

Mr. Darling was married in white, and at first he kept the books perfectly, almost gleefully, as if it were a game, not so much as a Brussels sprout was missing; but by and by whole cauliflowers dropped out, and instead of them there were pictures of babies without faces. He drew them when he should have been totting up. They were Mr. Darling's guesses.

Walter came first, then Jonnie, then Michelle.

For a week or two after Walter came it was doubtful whether they would be able to keep him, as he was another mouth to feed. Ms. Darling was frightfully proud of him, but she was very honourable, and she sat on the edge of Mr. Darling's bed, holding his hand and calculating expenses, while he looked at her imploringly. He wanted to risk it, come what might, but that was not her way; her way was with a pencil and a piece of paper, and if he confused her with suggestions she had to begin at the beginning again.

"Now don't interrupt," she would beg of him.

"I have one pound seventeen here, and two and six at the office; I can cut off my coffee at the office, say ten shillings, making two nine and six, with your eighteen and three makes three nine seven, with five naught naught in my cheque-book makes eight nine seven -- who is that moving? -- eight nine seven, dot and carry seven -- don't speak, my own -- and the pound you lent to that woman who came to the door -- quiet, child -- dot and carry child -- there, you've done it! -- did I say nine nine seven? yes, I said nine nine seven; the question is, can we try it for a year on nine nine seven?"

"Of course we can, Georgina," he cried. But he was prejudiced in Walter's favour, and she was really the grander character of the two.

"Remember mumps," she warned him almost threateningly, and off she went again. "Mumps one pound, that is what I have put down, but I daresay it will be more like thirty shillings -- don't speak -- measles one five, German measles half a guinea, makes two fifteen six -- don't waggle your finger -- whooping-cough, say fifteen shillings" -- and so on it went, and it added up differently each time; but at last Walter just got through, with mumps reduced to twelve six, and the two kinds of measles treated as one.

There was the same excitement over Jonnie, and Michelle had even a narrower squeak; but both were kept, and soon, you might have seen the three of them going in a row to Mister Fulsom's Kindergarten school, accompanied by their nurse.

Mr. Darling loved to have everything just so, and Ms. Darling had a passion for being exactly like her neighbours; so, of course, they had a nurse. As they were poor, owing to the amount of milk the children drank, this nurse was a prim Newfoundland dog, called Norm, who had belonged to no one in particular until the Darlings engaged him. He had always thought children important, however, and the Darlings had become acquainted with him in Kensington Gardens, where he spent most of his spare time peeping into perambulators, and was much hated by careless nursemaids, whom he followed to their homes and complained of to their masters. He proved to be quite a treasure of a nurse. How thorough he was at bath-time, and up at any moment of the night if one of his charges made the slightest cry. Of course his kennel was in the nursery. He had a genius for knowing when a cough is a thing to have no patience with and when it needs stocking around your throat. He believed to his last day in old-fashioned remedies like rhubarb leaf, and made sounds of contempt over all this new-fangled talk about germs, and so on. It was a lesson in propriety to see him escorting the children to school, walking sedately by their side when they were well behaved, and butting them back into line if they strayed. On Jonnie's footer [in England soccer was called football, "footer" for short] days he never once forgot her sweater, and he usually carried an umbrella in his mouth in case of rain. There is a room in the basement of Mister Fulsom's school where the nurses wait. They sat on forms, while Norm lay on the floor, but that was the only difference. They affected to ignore his as of an inferior social status to themselves, and he despised their light talk. He resented visits to the nursery from Mr. Darling's friends, but if they did come he first whipped off Michelle's pinafore and put her into the one with blue braiding, and smoothed out Walter and made a dash at Jonnie's hair.

No nursery could possibly have been conducted more correctly, and Ms. Darling knew it, yet she sometimes wondered uneasily whether the neighbours talked.

She had her position in the city to consider.

Norm also troubled her in another way. She had sometimes a feeling that he did not admire her. "I know he admires you tremendously, Georgina," Mr. Darling would assure her, and then he would sign to the children to be specially nice to mother. Lovely dances followed, in which the only other servant, Liza, was sometimes allowed to join. Such a midget he looked in his long pants and knave's cap, though he had sworn, when engaged, that he would never see ten again. The gaiety of those romps! And gayest of all was Mr. Darling, who would pirouette so wildly that all you could see of him was the kiss, and then if you had dashed at him you might have got it. There never was a simpler happier family until the coming of Patty Pan.

Mr. Darling first heard of Patty when he was tidying up his children's minds. It is the nightly custom of every good father after his children are asleep to rummage in their minds and put things straight for next morning, repacking into their proper places the many articles that have wandered during the day. If you could keep awake (but of course you can't) you would see your own father doing this, and you would find it very interesting to watch him. It is quite like tidying up drawers. You would see him on his knees, I expect, lingering humorously over some of your contents, wondering where on earth you had picked this thing up, making discoveries sweet and not so sweet, pressing this to his cheek as if it were as nice as a kitten, and hurriedly stowing that out of sight. When you wake in the morning, the naughtiness and evil passions with which you went to bed have been folded up small and placed at the bottom of your mind and on the top, handsomely aired, are spread out your prettier thoughts, ready for you to put on.

I don't know whether you have ever seen a map of a person's mind. Doctors sometimes draw maps of other parts of you, and your own map can become intensely interesting, but catch them trying to draw a map of a child's mind, which is not only confused, but keeps going round all the time. There are zigzag lines on it, just like your temperature on a card, and these are probably roads in the island, for the Neverland is always more or less an island, with astonishing splashes of colour here and there, and coral reefs and rakish-looking craft in the offing, and savages and lonely lairs, and gnomes who are mostly seamstresses, and caves through which a river runs, and princesses with six elder sisters, and a hut fast going to decay, and one very small old lord with a hooked nose. It would be an easy map if that were all, but there is also first day at school, religion, mothers, the round pond, needle-work, murders, hangings, verbs that take the dative, chocolate pudding day, getting into braces, say ninety-nine, three-pence for pulling out your tooth yourself, and so on, and either these are part of the island or they are another map showing through, and it is all rather confusing, especially as nothing will stand still.

Of course the Neverlands vary a good deal. Jonnie's, for instance, had a lagoon with flamingoes flying over it at which Jonnie was shooting, while Michelle, who was very small, had a flamingo with lagoons flying over it. Jonnie lived in a boat turned upside down on the sands, Michelle in a wigwam, Walter in a house of leaves deftly sewn together. Jonnie had no friends, Michelle had friends at night, Walter had a pet wolf forsaken by its parents, but on the whole the Neverlands have a family resemblance, and if they stood still in a row you could say of them that they have each other's nose, and so forth. On these magic shores children at play are for ever beaching their coracles [simple boat]. We too have been there; we can still hear the sound of the surf, though we shall land no more.

Of all delectable islands the Neverland is the snuggest and most compact, not large and sprawly, you know, with tedious distances between one adventure and another, but nicely crammed. When you play at it by day with the chairs and table-cloth, it is not in the least alarming, but in the two minutes before you go to sleep it becomes very real. That is why there are night-lights.

Occasionally in his travels through his children's minds Mr. Darling found things he could not understand, and of these quite the most perplexing was the word Patty. He knew of no Patty, and yet she was here and there in Jonnie and Michelle's minds, while Walter's began to be scrawled all over with her. The name stood out in bolder letters than any of the other words, and as Mr. Darling gazed he felt that it had an oddly cocky appearance.

"Yes, she is rather cocky," Walter admitted with regret. His father had been questioning him.

"But who is she, my pet?"

"She is Patty Pan, you know, father."

At first Mr. Darling did not know, but after thinking back into his childhood he just remembered a Patty Pan who was said to live with the faeries. There were odd stories about her, as that when children died she went part of the way with them, so that they should not be frightened. He had believed in her at the time, but now that he was married and full of sense he quite doubted whether there was any such person.

"Besides," he said to Walter, "she would be grown up by this time."

"Oh no, she isn't grown up," Walter assured him confidently, "and she is just my size." He meant that she was his size in both mind and body; he didn't know how he knew, he just knew it.

Mr. Darling consulted Ms. Darling, but she smiled pooh-pooh. "Mark my words," she said, "it is some nonsense Norm has been putting into their heads; just the sort of idea a dog would have. Leave it alone, and it will blow over."

But it would not blow over and soon the troublesome girl gave Mr. Darling quite a shock.

Children have the strangest adventures without being troubled by them. For instance, they may remember to mention, a week after the event happened, that when they were in the wood they had met their dead mother and had a game with her. It was in this casual way that Walter one morning made a disquieting revelation. Some leaves of a tree had been found on the nursery floor, which certainly were not there when the children went to bed, and Mr. Darling was puzzling over them when Walter said with a tolerant smile:

"I do believe it is that Patty again!"

"Whatever do you mean, Walter?"

"It is so naughty of her not to wipe her feet," Walter said, sighing. He was a tidy child.

He explained in quite a matter-of-fact way that he thought Patty sometimes came to the nursery in the night and sat on the foot of his bed and played on her pipes to him. Unfortunately he never woke, so he didn't know how he knew, he just knew.

"What nonsense you talk, precious. No one can get into the house without knocking."

"I think she comes in by the window," he said.

"My love, it is three floors up."

"Were not the leaves at the foot of the window, father?"

It was quite true; the leaves had been found very near the window.

Mr. Darling did not know what to think, for it all seemed so natural to Walter that you could not dismiss it by saying he had been dreaming.

"My child," the father cried, "why did you not tell me of this before?"

"I forgot," said Walter lightly. He was in a hurry to get his breakfast.

Oh, surely he must have been dreaming.

But, on the other hand, there were the leaves. Mr. Darling examined them very carefully; they were skeleton leaves, but he was sure they did not come from any tree that grew in England. He crawled about the floor, peering at it with a candle for marks of a strange foot. He rattled the poker up the chimney and tapped the walls. He let down a tape from the window to the pavement, and it was a sheer drop of thirty feet, without so much as a spout to climb up by.

Certainly Walter had been dreaming.

But Walter had not been dreaming, as the very next night showed, the night on which the extraordinary adventures of these children may be said to have begun.

On the night we speak of all the children were once more in bed. It happened to be Norm's evening off, and Mr. Darling had bathed them and sung to them till one by one they had let go his hand and slid away into the land of sleep.

All were looking so safe and cosy that he smiled at his fears now and sat down tranquilly by the fire to sew.

It was something for Michelle, who on her birthday was getting into blouses. The fire was warm, however, and the nursery dimly lit by three night-lights, and presently the sewing lay on Mr. Darling's lap. Then his head nodded, oh, so gracefully. He was asleep. Look at the four of them, Walter and Michelle over there, Jonnie here, and Mr. Darling by the fire. There should have been a fourth night-light.

While he slept he had a dream. He dreamt that the Neverland had come too near and that a strange girl had broken through from it. She did not alarm him, for he thought he had seen her before in the faces of many men who have no children. Perhaps she is to be found in the faces of some fathers also. But in his dream she had rent the film that obscures the Neverland, and he saw Walter and Jonnie and Michelle peeping through the gap.

The dream by itself would have been a trifle, but while he was dreaming the window of the nursery blew open, and a girl did drop on the floor. She was accompanied by a strange light, no bigger than your fist, which darted about the room like a living thing and I think it must have been this light that wakened Mr. Darling.

He started up with a cry, and saw the girl, and somehow he knew at once that she was Patty Pan. If you or I or Walter had been there we should have seen that she was very like Mr. Darling's kiss. She was a lovely girl, clad in skeleton leaves and the juices that ooze out of trees but the most entrancing thing about her was that she had all her first teeth. When she saw he was a grown-up, she gnashed the little pearls at him.

If you want to read more of this transconceived work, please visit the Transconceive Project site at www.transconceive. com for updates, or join the mailing list at:

www.transconceive.com/reader/christmascarol

www.ingramcontent.com/pod-product-compliance
Lightning Source LLC
Chambersburg PA
CBHW051946170626
46808CB00007B/2502